TWO CENTS OF DOOM

KARI LEE TOWNSEND

All rights reserved.

No part of this publication may be sold, copied, distributed, reproduced or transmitted in any form or by any means, mechanical or digital, including photocopying and recording or by any information storage and retrieval system without the prior written permission of both the publisher, Oliver Heber Books and the author, Kari Lee Townsend, except in the case of brief quotations embodied in critical articles and reviews.

PUBLISHER'S NOTE: This is a work of fiction. Names, characters, places, and incidents either are the product of the author's imagination or are used fictitiously. Any resemblance to actual persons, living or dead, business establishments, events, or locales is entirely coincidental.

Copyright © Kari Lee Townsend

Published by Oliver-Heber Books

0 9 8 7 6 5 4 3 2 1

CHAPTER 1

"Welcome back, Kalli." Detective Stevens took my hand and then kissed my cheek as a summer breeze carried the smell of fresh-cut grass and flowers past my nose. We stood at the edge of his ma's brand-new house, sneaking in a moment alone before everyone else saw us.

I inhaled deep and smiled up at him. "Thanks."

He was so handsome, dressed in khaki's and a sky-blue polo shirt that brought out the sapphire blue of his eyes. He was tall with thick, wavy, coffee-colored hair, olive skin and a heavily whiskered face. His piercing eyes twinkled before he leaned in to whisper, "I missed you," into my ear while still holding my hand, and I read his mind. *If you give me a chance, I'll be happy to show you just how much.*

"I missed you, too," I whispered back, then took a step away, letting go of his hand and flushing over his thoughts as I discreetly applied my ever-present hand sanitizer to my palms, spinning my fidget ring three times. I smoothed my gray business suit, feeling awkward, never having successfully dated. With everything so new and still up in the air between us, I didn't quite know how to act around him. It didn't help that I hadn't seen him in weeks.

He started filling me in on what had been happening in our small Connecticut town, Clearview, while I was away, but my mind kept wandering. Ever since I fell and hit my head, I'd been able to read people's minds. It was because of this gift that I'd been able to kiss a man and not think about all the germs we were exchanging. Nik's thoughts made me stay out of my own head and enjoy the moment.

He was a complex man. I'd come to know him as Nik the nice guy, Nikos the smug Greek, and the all-business Detective Stevens. One minute I wanted to smack him, and the next he made me weak in the knees. I hadn't told him about my gift because I didn't want him to think I was even stranger than he already thought I was.

The last time I saw him we'd agreed to give dating a shot. But first, I'd had to go to New York City for several meetings with the head of Interludes regarding my new collection of Kalli Originals lingerie. Thanks to my best friend, Jaz Alvarez, letting me display my collection in her boutique, Full Disclosure, I'd been discovered by Interludes. Having them carry my line was a dream come true. Not to mention, it allowed me to pay my part of the rent on the half a house I shared with Jaz. Detective Dreamy rented the other half of the house.

I loved my adoptive Greek family, but living at home had become unbearable. Ma was constantly trying to *fix* me and marry me off so I would give her grandbabies. My gaze locked with my handsome detective as he continued to talk. I used to think marriage and motherhood wasn't in my future, but for the first time in my life, I had hope. Nik was only half

Greek, but apparently that was Greek enough for my desperate Ma.

"Everything okay?" He raised a brow at me with a half-smile. "You're staring at me like you're in a daze. Did you hear anything I said?"

"Sorry. My mind is all over the place." I could feel my cheeks heat.

His eyes softened. "It's okay. I'm just glad to have you home."

"Me, too." A sense of peace filled me as we started walking into the yard.

"Kalliope Ballas, you're home!" Aunt Tasoula squealed, heading in my direction with her arms open wide.

I jumped. So much for peace, but family was family, no matter how crazy.

Aunt Tasoula was my ma's sister, but they didn't look anything alike. She owned a hair salon, was half my ma's size, and tried to look much younger with black hair that was way too long and clothes that were far too tight.

She tsked. "Look at these split ends." She picked up a strand of my thick golden blond hair that had fallen out of my signature chignon, inspecting the ends. "You come to my salon. I give you a trim." *Some lowlights would do her good. She's way too pale for a Greek.*

Over my dead body would I let her touch my hair with chemicals. I shivered over the thought of Parabens, Formaldehyde, and Phthalates to name a few of many harmful ingredients found in hair products. I could become infertile, lose my hair, develop asthma and maybe even cancer just so my hair would smell good and look three-dimensional. And to think what it might do to my brain. That had already taken enough abuse, thank you very much.

I gave her a quick hug and stepped back the second she let me go, happy not to read her mind anymore. "Thank you for the offer, but I'm so busy right now with my new clothing line finally out."

"Ah, about that." She looked around and lowered her voice. "I, um, have a friend who would like to place an order on the line."

"You mean an online order?"

"Yes, that's what I said." She frowned. "Put some aloe in your ears. That will help your hearing."

"I'll be happy to help you with your online order." I lowered my voice to match hers. "For your friend, of course."

"Good girl." She patted my had. "I'll be in touch." She looked around the busy back yard again. "I trust you'll be discreet."

"Always." I smiled knowingly. Half my family had a *friend* who wanted to place an order who happened to wear their exact size. They all loved my Kalli Original lingerie, even though none of them would ever admit it.

"My baby!" My ma, Ophelia Ballas, rushed to my side and inspected every inch of me, her big poof of teased black hair not moving an inch. "You were gone so long. What did they do to you? Your suit is baggy. You're too thin. Come with me." She took me by the arm, her satin blouse billowing and polyester pants swishing as she pulled me toward the gazebo in Chloe Steven's brand-new back yard.

I gave Nik an apologetic look and received a wink in return.

My cousin Yanni owned a landscaping business called Yanni's Yards. Ma had told me he'd hired a new guy. Looking around, I was impressed. The man had talent. It wasn't easy landscaping anything for a Greek Sunday brunch and not have it be over the top, but it was clear he had an artistic eye.

"I knew letting you go off to the big city alone was a bad idea," Ma interrupted my train of thought. "First, you make scandalous lingerie, and now you no eat." She shook her beehive nest of hair. *I'll put some aloe in her tea. That'll fix her right up.*

I gently pulled my arm from my ma's grasp so I didn't have to hear her thoughts lecture me, and no way was I drinking aloe. I sighed as my stomach turned over. The city had been a nice break from my big fat Greek life.

Nik knew exactly how I felt. His ma was Greek and had divorced his father years ago because he *wasn't*, blaming that for all their problems. She was all class and sophistication, with her trendy chic haircut and clothes, but she schemed as much as my ma did. She'd moved to Clearview Connecticut to be closer to her only child just as soon as she'd found a suitable house. This Sunday brunch was the first in her yard to christen the move before Nik's extended Pagonis family returned to their homes.

I had missed mass at our Greek Orthodox Church today—a sin in my pop's eyes—due to horrendous traffic making me late. So, the second I crossed the town line, I'd headed right to brunch before I'd sinned any further. I mean, I hadn't missed much. Well, okay...I admittedly missed a certain dreamy detective more than I'd thought possible.

"There you are, Roomie." Jaz hooked my arm with hers and pulled me away from the mamas. *Thank the Lord Boomer isn't Greek. There's not enough Ouzo on the planet that would help me survive a family like that.*

Jaz was tall and perfectly proportioned, with thick honey brown curls and amber eyes. She had her investment banker father's brains and her model mother's looks, but after seeing how her mother's wandering eye had hurt her father, she'd vowed never to fall in love. That was before Detective Boomer Matheson had been relentless in convincing her otherwise. With his unruly russet hair, hazel eyes, and long lean body, he wasn't her usual type. She normally went for brainless blond beefcakes, but Boomer was her feisty equal. When they weren't trying to kill each other, they were head over heels, and I couldn't be happier for her.

"Thank you, but do you mind?" I looked at our looped arms.

"Whoops, sorry, I keep forgetting about your gift." She dropped my arm and adjusted the straps of a floral sundress, undoubtedly one of her summer finds for her boutique. She had a great eye for fashion, outdoing the only other competition in town at Vixen's.

Jaz was the only one I had told about my mind-reading ability. For starters, it had first happened in her store and had been hard to hide from her since she was the one who found me on the floor. Not to mention, I had needed at least one person to talk to about it before I lost my mind completely. Who better than my best friend to help keep me sane?

"You seem happy." My gaze followed Boomer as he headed over to Nik.

"I am." She giggled. "Deliriously so, for now, anyway. Ask me tomorrow, and the story might be different. My man certainly keeps me on my toes."

"I'm happy for you, Jaz. You deserve this."

"Thanks." Her gaze shot to Nik, deep in conversation with Boomer, then back to me. "Speaking of men and happiness...any updates?"

Heat crept up my neck as I remembered Nik's whispered words that he'd missed me and couldn't wait to show me how much. I pulled the collar of my blouse away from my throat and fanned my neck. "I'm not sure. I mean, we definitely have chemistry. That was evident before I left for New York City. He did say he wanted to take me out on an official date when I got back, but I know he just got out of a relationship only a couple of months ago, right before moving here. Up until that time, I didn't think a relationship was even possible for me. I don't want to rush into anything, and I especially don't want to be someone's rebound."

"So don't." Jaz lifted one delicate shoulder. "It's only a date, Kalli. We're not talking weddings and babies." Her gaze traveled to the food table. "The mamas, on the other hand, are on a mission for both."

I followed her line of sight and groaned. My ma and Nik's ma were huddled together with heads bent, discussing Lord only knew what, their hands moving as fast as their lips. They'd probably already planned the next five years of our lives when all I wanted to do was make it through the next five minutes. I liked Nik, I really did, but I couldn't shake the knot of unease in my stomach.

The gentle breeze turned to a gust of wind as it swirled into the back yard, blowing paper plates, napkins and cups off the food table beneath the gazebo. Marble statues and an impressive water fountain were soon covered. Nik's relatives mixed with mine as they ran about duct taping everything down in an attempt to save brunch.

Children laughed in glee, and my cousin Frona skipped about with her crooked ponytails, singing,

"Ring around the rosy, paper plates a blowy," as she snatched items from the air in glee. Frona was my age but had fallen off an apple cart years ago and hadn't been the same since. She was happy, safe, and cared for by my family, but my ma had checked my pupils every day since my fall. She was terrified my fate would be the same, especially since I was her only child. She got upset that I wouldn't let her duct tape my ears. I'd had to draw the line somewhere. My life was crazy. Not much shocked me anymore.

Suddenly two women came barreling around the corner. One was most definitely a Greek mama, judging by the dark hair, fierce determination blazing from her eyes, and firm grip she had on a younger stunning version of herself. The unease in my gut grew to full blown acid reflux, making me worry my esophagus would be fried. I sensed there wasn't enough aloe or duct tape in the universe to save brunch, much less anything else at this point. My gut had never been wrong, and this time was no exception.

The mama and daughter came to a stop right in the center of the yard, and everyone froze, all eyes trained on the dramatic duo. The mama looked around, her furious gaze finally spotting who she sought, and my heart dropped.

Detective Nik Stevens.

Nik frowned. "Ariana, what are you doing here?"

The younger woman wouldn't quite look at him.

His gaze turned to the older woman beside her. "Penelope?"

"It's Mrs. Drakos to you."

"Fine, *Mrs. Drakos*, but I can't imagine why you're here. Your daughter and I broke up months ago."

"Not before you left her with a little gift. If her father were still alive, he would kill you." She made the sign of the cross. "I'm all she has, and I want to know what you're going to do about it."

"Do about what?" Nik rubbed his temples. "I'm afraid I don't know what are you talking about?"

Penelope Drakos snapped her spine straight. "My precious daughter is pregnant, and you're the papa."

Nik gaped.

Chloe fainted.

Chaos ensued.

I guess weddings and babies were in the future after all...just not in mine.

~

"I DON'T KNOW if I'll ever get over my shock." I looked at Jaz as we sat on our back deck that evening, sipping wine. We'd changed into yoga pants and t-shirts. It was a comfort sort of night.

Jaz owned a big old colonial house with a huge fenced-in backyard on Picture Perfect Drive—a dead end road just off of Main Street. She'd had carpenters split the house into two halves, insisting she didn't need that much space. I couldn't afford to rent the other half by myself yet, and I was determined not to take charity from anyone, so I paid to live with her. She rented the other half of the house to Detective Stevens. I had to stop thinking of him as Nik, or I would fall apart.

"You and me both. What a mess." She looked out over the yard.

Priscilla, aka Ms. Priss, perched on the railing, turning up her nose to the huge, sloppy St. Bernard staring at her from the other side of the fence that separated our half of the lawn from the detective's. My calico cat was about as prissy, picky and finicky as they came. She tolerated his dog Wolfgang occasionally, but for the most part she teased the poor, slobbery, silly, goofball relentlessly. He didn't care. Every day he came back for more torture, whining as he adored her from afar.

As for Wolfy and me, we had come to an understanding. If he kept his germ ridden saliva to himself and his wiggling fanny firmly planted on the ground, then I would pet his massive head briefly. Followed quickly by a thorough scrubbing of my hands with my hand sanitizer, of course. However, I couldn't bring myself to go near anything belonging to the detective after the brunch bombshell that had been dropped earlier today.

"A baby? That changes everything." I kicked off my flipflops to prop my bare feet on the clean stool in front of my Adirondack chair, where they were safe from splinters. I wasn't taking any chances. Anything that pierces the skin can create a point of entry for microbes from outside the body, leading to horrifying infections.

"I have to admit, I didn't see that one coming." Jaz took a sip of her wine, completely barefoot without a care in the world. She always put slippers on when reentering the house because she knew I would follow her everywhere with a mop if she didn't. "I'm all for having fun, but Nik is a smart man," she added. "How could he let something like this happen?"

"I have no clue." I took a deep breath and frowned down at my glass, the wine tasting spoiled all of a sudden. "But it's not my problem." I stared out at the woods out behind our fence, watching some crows fight off a hawk who was probably after their young.

"I thought you were going on a date with Nik."

"Not anymore. Not after this. I'm a firm believer in signs, and this is a big one." I swirled the wine in my glass, fascinated by its golden color that was a pretty close match to my hair. I set my glass down, feeling defeated. "She's full Greek and an absolute goddess. I can't compete with that."

At that moment, Detective Dreamy walked out onto his back deck and called Wolfgang to come inside. His gaze met mine and locked. He hesitated like he wanted to say something, so I looked away. I couldn't get in the middle of his mess right now, no matter how tempting he was. I didn't look up until I heard his screen door close.

"You really don't know how beautiful you are, my friend. Trust me, you have way more to offer than her. After you left brunch, Nik's ma and Penelope got into a yelling match and everyone started gossiping. Nik's family filled in your family with plenty. I guess Chloe never liked Ariana. She didn't trust her and didn't think she was the right woman for Nik, but Nik's a nice guy. He didn't want to hurt Ariana's feelings and was just having fun anyway."

The moment after the bombshell had been dropped, I'd lost my appetite and hightailed it out of there, not caring to hear anymore. But I had to admit, I was curious now. "Then why did they break up?"

"I guess when he found out she used to date a guy involved with the mob and lied about it to him, he realized it didn't look good on him since he's a cop. He was the one who ended things. Let's just say Ariana didn't take it well. I don't think she's used to anyone dumping her. Her ma took it even worse. Chloe was relieved to be rid of them, but now her worst nightmare has come true. Poor woman. I'm sure Nik will do the right thing by the baby, but that doesn't mean he has to marry Ariana."

I was already shaking my head. "It doesn't matter either way. I have my new lingerie line to focus on. I can't afford to get distracted by getting caught up in a bunch of drama. Nik was the only guy who didn't care about my quirks, and the only guy whose kisses made me stop thinking completely, but whatever was between us is now over, ending before it even started. I should have known things were too good to be true."

"Aw, Kalli, I'm sorry. I just want to see you happy." Jaz squeezed my hand, and I smiled, then quickly let go. "What are you going to do?"

"What I should have done from the beginning. Mind my own business." I slipped my shoes back on, picked up my wine glass and scooped up my cat, then gave one last glance at Detective Dreamy's deck before heading inside to pour myself a different glass of therapy. Maybe something stronger.

My sketchbook lay open on my kitchen table with a brand-new design I'd finished this morning. My first ever Kalli Original I'd designed specifically for myself with Nikos Stevens in mind. I groaned.

Minding my own business just might be harder than I thought.

CHAPTER 2

One week later, I was in the loft of Full Disclosure, working on my designs. Jaz's clothing boutique was my second home. Located in the business district, it was a high-end clothing store that people from all over frequented.

Debbie, the fashion designer intern she'd hired, sat on a throw pillow on a stool behind the register cashing people out. Jaz wanted her to learn every aspect of the fashion business, and it was nice to have the help as her business had grown. There was a burgundy microfiber sofa in the sitting area next to the dressing rooms with decorative pin-striped pillows and a matching loveseat filled with shoppers. Soft music played through the sound system, and the boutique smelled of lavender.

Jaz had a full cleaning crew, but I still secretly sanitized the furniture every chance I got. At least my loft studio was spotless, just the way I liked it, with a hand sanitizer stand at the top of the stairs just in case. No one was allowed up there. That was my only request when it came to my sanctuary, and Jaz had been gracious enough to give me that. Right now, more than ever, I needed a place to escape to so I could get out of my head and do what I loved best.

Living next door to the detective made it difficult to avoid him, but so far, I had managed to do just that. I'd seen Ariana's car parked in his driveway nearly every day. During that fateful brunch, her ma had been the force to reckon with. According to the rumor mill, Ariana had gotten over her quiet awkwardness and had been pursuing Nik relentlessly this past week. It wouldn't be long before she wore the man down. I couldn't help feeling a little sorry for him. It had to be exhausting.

The bells on the front door of Jaz's boutique chimed. I peeked over the new, fully reinforced railing of the loft. Jaz had spared no expense after my fall. Speaking of forces to be reckoned with. Ariana and her ma, Penelope, breezed through the door with confidence rolling off them in waves, which was something I was in short supply of these days. Jaz joined them with a smile, always the professional. They were studying Jaz's hot summer finds. I couldn't blame them. Jaz had a great eye.

Ariana wore a pretty pale pink sundress in the latest fashion, looking as if she'd just stepped off a runway. Her hair fell in thick, soft curls to the middle of her perfect back. Her skin glowed a perfect shade of tan, and her figure was one every woman would envy. The woman was literally flawless. I couldn't help being a little jealous.

I sucked in a sharp breath when I saw her stop in front of my Kalli's Originals display. Jaz gave her a beaming smile, talking animatedly for several minutes, then she pointed up toward me. With no time to duck, I locked eyes with Ariana. She smiled wide as she gave me a wave and motioned for me to come join them.

Just great. So much for escaping.

Pasting on my own practiced professional smile, I made my way down the stairs to the store below. I tucked a strand of hair back into my classic chignon then smoothed the front of my wrinkle free skirt before coming to a stop beside them.

"This is Kalli Ballas, the designer of these fabulous pieces." Jaz swept her hand down over my lingerie display as if she were a model showcasing a prize on a game show. "Aren't they delicious?" Jaz was my biggest supporter, and I loved her for it, but right now I wanted to disappear.

"They're something." Penelope studied me critically, as if looking for a weakness. I wasn't the enemy, yet she was sizing me up as if I were. I couldn't figure her out, but then it dawned on me. She'd probably heard about my very public kiss with a certain Detective Dreamy and viewed me as competition for her daughter. If she only knew I'd thrown in my white towel the second the word baby was mentioned.

"Thank you," I replied, then turned my attention onto Ariana. "I hear congratulations are in order."

She stared at me with a blank expression, looking confused for a moment, until her ma coughed. "Ah, yes." She dropped her hands to her flat stomach and smiled all cat-that-ate-the-canary like. "Thank you. We're very excited."

I couldn't help wonder who *we* were.

Move on, Kalli, I lectured myself. "Is there something I can help you with?"

"Actually, yes," Mrs. Drakos chimed in. "I guess you're the right person for the job." She looked me over in a calculated way, then straightened to her full height before adding, "Ariana needs a wedding trousseau."

I swallowed my gum, horrified over what part of my insides it might stick to. It was a known fact that the human body couldn't digest chewing gum. I gagged. "What was that?" I finally got out between coughs.

"Haven't you heard?" Ariana's eyes widened a little too innocently. "Nikos and I are engaged to be married."

And there it was.

Jaz went into a choking fit this time. "Excuse me," she wheezed. "A customer needs me." She waved to Mrs. Flannigan, one of her regular customers who'd just walked in, and hurried off a little too hastily.

So much for my biggest supporter. My best friend had abandoned ship the second she realized it was sinking, leaving me to drown alone.

"Wow, that is—" *fast* "—wonderful news." I rubbed my aching stomach, wishing I could jump ship and put myself out of my misery. Instead, I plastered on my best game face. "When would you need something by?"

"The sooner the better, I would say. You know, given the situation, and all," her ma said, her face looking pinched. All Greek mamas wanted grandbabies, but none of them that I'd ever met enjoyed a scandal.

Ariana rolled her eyes. "Relax, Ma, you're so dramatic. I'm not even showing." She grinned at me devilishly. "It can take five or six months for a first-time mother to show. Let's make it something vintage. Heirloom quality. I want to make sure it's a night my Nikos will never forget." She obviously enjoyed the effect her words had on me.

I never could hide my emotions very well.

A whiff of her strong perfume hit me in the face, and I felt sick. I looked at my watch, trying not to vomit up the acid churning in my stomach. "I'm sorry to cut you short, but I have an appointment. Why don't you email me what you have in mind, and I'll come up with some sketches for you to choose from. Will that work?"

"That sounds perfect." Ariana held out her hand, and I had no choice but to shake hers if I didn't want to appear rude. *Oh, honey, did you really think you stood a chance against me? Nikos is mine and always has been. Little girl. You'll never—*

I yanked my hand away and tried not to fist my palm.

Both Ariana and her ma eyed me suspiciously.

"Sorry, cramp." I shook my hand. "Gotta run. I'll be in touch." I hurried off, making a beeline for the front door as I scrubbed my palm with hand sanitizer, not caring a whit if they saw me or not. The nerve of that woman. She was the rude one. I couldn't understand what on earth a man like Detective Stevens saw in a conniving woman like that, but it didn't matter now anyway.

He was her Nikos and most definitely not my Nik.

Avoiding him was one thing. But how in the name of Zeus was I going to survive designing his *fiancé's* lingerie when just over a week ago I'd designed one for myself with him in mind. Most of the time, my family drove me crazy, but one thing was certain. They were always there for me if I ever needed anything. Right now, I needed comfort and knew just where to find it.

Aphrodite's.

"My poor baby." My ma gave me a quick hug, knowing better than to linger, thank goodness.

I wasn't so much worried about germs from her food splattered apron for once, as I was more worried about her thoughts. Right now, I just needed her comfort and familiar homey smells, not her lectures.

"Here. You eat. I made your favorites." She slid a plate of Soutzoukakia, aka Greek meatballs and pastitsio, also known as Greek lasagna, in front of me, followed by melt-in-your-mouth Greek olive and onion bread.

For once, I didn't argue. I ate.

Aphrodite's was my parents' other baby. The goddess of love, beauty, and all things Greek filled every inch of space, with plenty of marble statues scattered about just short of overkill. Everyone loved Aphrodite's with her beautiful Greek culture on display and food prepared with skill and pride.

My cousin, Eleni, worked at my parents' restaurant as a waitress, and her sister Frona was the dishwasher. When they could keep her in the back, that is. Eleni adjusted her long black ponytail then scrubbed her hands three times before picking out a pastry with a clean napkin, placing it on a sanitized plate, and then setting it on my table as she passed by. She blew me a kiss, and my heart squeezed tight.

She knew me so well.

Even Frona refrained from skipping about and playing with the salt and pepper shakers as if she sensed I wasn't up for any more shenanigans. She only bounced once before slipping in the back like a good girl. I loved my family so much.

I sighed, frustrated with Nik. I'd been so excited to return from the city after a successful launch of my new lingerie line, thrilled to have a summer filled with more excitement and fun than I'd had in far too long. Why'd he have to go and ruin everything? I should have known taking a chance on a relationship hadn't been a good idea.

Romance never worked out for me.

The door to the restaurant opened and in walked the object of my thoughts. My stomach filled with butterflies, ignoring my brain. He looked around the restaurant intensely, until he spotted me. Then his piercing blue gaze held mine captive as he took long, purposeful strides in my direction. I gathered my trash as quickly as I could and stood, ready to make my escape out the back. Before I could take a single step, he reached out and snagged my arms, sending a little thrill through me.

I scowled over my traitorous body.

"Oh, no, you don't, Kalliope Ballas." He gave me a frustrated look. "No more avoiding me. I need to talk to you." He took a moment to just breathe. "I need to know you're okay. This has to be affecting you."

"I'm fine." I started to pull away, but something in his face made me pause. *Please, Kalli, just hear me out. Not knowing how you feel is killing me. I need you to hear my side. Hell, I just need you.* Well, shoot, that was my undoing. Helpless to do otherwise, I sat back down, and his arms fell away.

The restaurant grew deathly quiet. All eyes were on us. Pop and Papou appeared from the kitchen, meeting my eyes in question. I signaled I was okay, and everyone resumed eating as if nothing had happened.

I focused on Nik. "I'm listening."

Relief transformed his face, and for the first time, I noticed the little lines of stress at the corners of his eyes. He looked exhausted. He scrubbed a hand through his unruly curls then over his face in desperate need of a shave. "I don't know where to start."

My heart couldn't help but melt. I actually had the urge to hug him. That was a first. "How about you start at the beginning?" I'd heard the rumors, but wanted to hear his side of the story.

"Okay, so I met Ariana years ago. She's a realtor and helped me find an apartment. She was beautiful and feisty and fun. Ma was driving me crazy, trying to fix me up with woman after woman. I wasn't ready to settle down, and certainly not with a woman of my ma's choosing." He grunted.

I nodded, smiling a little and listening patiently, totally relating to where he was coming from. "Go on."

"Ariana was a little loud for my taste, but she was Greek. I thought that would be enough to keep my ma off my back." He shrugged. "It was at first."

I played with my napkin. "What happened to change that?"

"Ma kept catching Ariana in lies." He took a long sip of the water Eleni had discreetly placed in front of him as if sensing he might need it. "As much as my ma wanted me to get married and give her grandbabies, she also wanted me to be happy. She's very protective of me since I'm an only child."

A small laugh slipped out. "I can definitely relate to that."

"Right?" He shook his head. "Anyway, she wouldn't stop pressuring me to break up with Ariana."

"Why didn't you if you weren't serious about her?" I studied him, genuinely curious as to how he really felt about her.

"I don't want you to think I stayed with Ariana because I was in love with her. I wasn't, but I knew Ma would start trying to fix me up again. It's exhausting fending off a Greek mama. You know that."

I was already nodding. "Yes, I do."

"Ari might not be marriage material, but she used to be fun at least."

"Then why break up at all?"

"My job." Sincerity filled his voice. "When I found out Ariana dated a man in the mob, I confronted her. She outright lied to my face, but I had proof. I knew I couldn't be associated with her anymore. Let's just say she doesn't handle rejection well."

"So I've heard." He'd confirmed everything Jaz had told me. I could live with that, but I couldn't understand how he could be so careless. He was a smart man. He *had* to know how A+B=C works. So, if he didn't want a C, then he shouldn't have combined A with B.

"You have the most expressive face. It's one of the things I like best about you. You don't play games, and I know exactly how you feel." His soft gaze turned frustrated. "I've been beating myself up for over a week." He rubbed his hands over his face. "I don't get it. I always use protection and am extremely careful for this very reason. At the end, we weren't even close. It's been a couple months, but that doesn't mean it isn't possible for her to be pregnant." He lifted his hands up. "I'm a man of honor. If it turns out the baby is mine, I will do the right thing by my child."

"Wait," I gaped at him, "*if?*"

"I don't trust Ariana one bit." He rubbed his neck as if trying to ease the tension. "I'm having a paternity test as soon as possible."

His words weren't making any sense. My head was swimming with confusion. "Then why on earth did you propose?"

Once more, the restaurant activity halted, forks raised halfway, and mouths as open as my Detective Dreamy's was.

His blue eyes narrowed. "Say what?" he finally managed to get out.

A screech rang out. "Nikos Stevens, are you absolutely crazy?" Chloe entered the restaurant just in time to hear her the news and stormed over to our table. "That woman is out to ruin you. *What* were you thinking?"

Nik's eyebrows shot sky high as he eyed us both as if we'd lost our minds. "I don't know what either of you are talking about."

"Ariana came into Full Disclosure this morning and asked me to make a wedding trousseau for her because you two are engaged," I said carefully to be sure he understood. "Her ma confirmed it."

The restaurant started buzzing with gossip.

Nik's chiseled features hardened as his intense eyes blazed. "You will do no such thing, Kalli. I promise you, we are not engaged. Baby or no baby, I would never ask Ariana to marry me. I don't love her." His anger-filled gaze bore into mine and softened for a moment as he added, "My heart—"

"Well, you might want to inform the Drakos women of that," I said, not ready to think about what the rest of his sentence might have been.

"Oh, you can bet *I'll* inform those monsters that no way in Mount Olympus will Nikos Stevens ever marry Ariana Drakos." Chloe raised her voice. "Over my dead body. I'll kill her or die trying before I ever let that happen."

She looked around the full restaurant that was suddenly all ears, staring at her as if they were statues in a wax museum. Flustered, she waved her hands in front of her and stormed out the front door. A sense of doom filled me as one thought rolled around in my brain like fifty-foot waves looking for a target....

What kind of damage was Hurricane Chloe about to unleash?

CHAPTER 3

Another week went by with me dodging a certain dreamy detective once more. I didn't know what else we possibly had to say to each other, and we weren't any closer to fixing this mess he was in. His family had extended their stay, rallying support around Nik in their attempt to undo the damage the Drakos women were unleashing on Clearview.

Meanwhile, Hurricane Chloe was growing in intensity.

The Dramatic Duo wouldn't take no for an answer, moving forward with wedding plans despite an unwilling groom. Both Penelope and Ariana were racking up a list of local enemies at an impressive speed. Nik was doing his best to keep the peace around town, but I could see the toll the drama was taking on him when he thought no one was watching.

I looked into the back yard and noticed Wolfgang wasn't there. Nik never veered from his routine. The rumor was Wolfgang didn't like Ariana, either. She'd tried to make Nik get rid of him back when they were dating. Instead, he'd gotten rid of her. Another point of contention between them, I was sure.

My cell phone rang, and I checked the caller ID then groaned. "Hi, Ma. What's up this time?"

"Can't a mama call her daughter without an ulterior motive?"

"A normal mama, maybe. My Greek ma? Not so much."

She tried to sound wounded over my words, but I knew better.

"Okay, Ma." *I'll play*, I thought. "How are you this fine morning?"

"Not so good." She sighed in dramatic fashion worthy of an Oscar. "This morning's not fine it turns out. My bunions are acting up something fierce. How am I supposed to work all day? It's all your Aunt Tasoula's fault for convincing me to wear those ridiculous pointy shoes. Feet are round, not pointy. A man must have designed those. Those torture devices made me look like a clown. I think she's jealous that my business is doing better than hers. My poor feet will never be the same again."

"You know she loves you, Ma. She's just always trying to do a makeover on everyone. Wrap your feet in aloe and duct tape. I'm sure that will fix them right up." I bit my bottom lip, but a little giggle slipped out.

"Are you cracking wise with me, Kalliope Mary Ballas?"

I crossed my fingers behind my back. "Never."

"Hmmm, I would hope not. You'll be sorry when I'm gone someday. You'll miss me. You'll see."

"You're going to outlive us all, Ma." She wasn't fooling anyone.

"I do have the good genes. Doctor LaLone always tells me so. You take after me. You got the good genes, too."

I was pretty sure genes didn't transfer through

adoption, but to say so to my ma would be blasphemy. "Lucky me," I safely responded instead. "Now, please, tell me why you really called?"

"You have no time for me. Oh, woe is me." I pictured her hand on her forehead through the phone and couldn't help but grin slightly. Just like that, she dropped the act and moved on. "Poor Chloe Stevens is not so good, either."

That erased the smile from my face, and I stood a little straighter. "What's wrong with Detective Stevens' ma?"

"We don't know. Her family are all here at the restaurant. They said she went to bed early last night with the bug. She didn't answer when they called her this morning to go to breakfast."

I relaxed. "I'm sure she's just sleeping in, Ma."

"Well, I would feel better checking in on her, but I'm too busy to leave the restaurant. This place would fall apart without me, bunions or not."

I took the not-so-subtle hint. "Would you like me to stop by her house on my way in to work?"

"Yes, and Kalliope, stop by Diner Delights and ask Kosmos and Silas for some of their chicken soup. That will fix her right up."

"Sure thing, Ma." I hung up, gathered my sketchbook, said goodbye to my cat who turned up her nose and ignored me, and headed outside.

"Perfect timing," Rex Drummond, our new mailman, said to me as he handed me my mail.

"Thanks, Mr. Drummond." I flipped through the mail eagerly, too excited to care that I didn't have my latex gloves on. Paper was filthy.

"Please, call me Rex," he said, but I wasn't really paying attention, distracted to see if the item I had been waiting for had arrived.

"Yes!" I squealed. "The new Interludes catalogue is here." I flipped the magazine open and laughed out loud with pure joy.

"I take it your negligees are in there?"

I blinked and looked up at him. He knew about my lingerie?

"Amos and Homer told me about your new line," he quickly verified, his cheeks flushing slightly pink. "Didn't want you to think I was a stalker or anything." He laughed uncomfortably. He was in his forties, of average height, with a slightly stocky build. He seemed like a nice enough guy, just a little socially awkward. "Welp. Gotta go. Need to finish my run before the storm hits." With a quick hop in his mail truck, he was gone.

What a funny little man, I thought, but then I noticed the horizon.

Storm clouds covered the sky with a gloomy gray, carrying the threat of a thunderstorm on the whipping wind, laden with moisture. I hurried over to my Prius, threw my mail on the seat, then pulled a sanitary wipe out of my purse to clean my hands. Hopping in my car, I headed downtown. A few minutes later, I pulled into my cousins' diner's parking lot and ducked inside, just as sprinkles started to fall from the sky. Mouth-watering smells filled the air of seasoned meats, cheeses, olives, soups, sandwiches, salads and desserts. My stomach growled.

Stepping up to the counter, I smiled at Eleanor and Olivia Bennett, Clearview's newest residents before Chloe Stevens had moved to town. The impeccable identical twins were in their sixties, with short, slicked-back, trendy gray hair. They were trying to decide where they wanted to retire before buying. They'd moved to town two months ago, rented a house off of Main Street, and had already become locals. The Gossip Queens seemed to know everything about everyone already.

No wonder my ma had become fast friends with them.

"Oh, Kalli, how's your mother's feet, dear?" Eleanor asked.

"My Pop will wrap them in duct tape. She'll be good as new in no time, but thank you for asking."

"Next time tell her to ask us if she needs any fashion advice," Olivia added. "It's what we do best."

Don't tell my aunt that, I thought, but I did have to admit the women were always dressed sharply from head to toe, accessories and all. "I will," I said. "It was good seeing you. I have to get some soup over to Chloe Stevens. She's not feeling well."

I waved to my cousin Kosmos. He was short, but built like a tank, with dark hair cropped tight and sleepy bedroom eyes that all the women fell for, but the man was oblivious to his charm. Ma had called ahead obviously, because Kosmos held up a container already filled and brought it over to his brother. Silas was the exact opposite. Tall with curly black hair and dimples, he used to flirt outrageously with all the women in town, no matter their age. Needless to say, their diner was doing very well.

"Chloe Stevens. Now there's a woman who knows about fashion and how to accessorize," Olivia pointed out, then her eyes widened and her lips formed an oh. "She's not feeling well?"

"Oh, dear me, let us know if there is anything we can do." Eleanor paid Silas for a tray of lamb gyros and ice teas.

"It's no wonder the poor thing is under the weather, given those awful Drakos women," Olivia added, stepping up to help her sister. "They won't leave the poor dear alone, cornering her in Sal's Supermarket and causing such a scene last night. Can you believe they demanded Chloe help pay for a wedding reception that may never happen? Why, it was downright scandalous the things they called her and her son."

"It was horrible enough to make anyone go a little crazy." Eleanor shook her head. "I don't blame Chloe for heading next door to Wilma's Wine & Spirits. Those two women are downright evil enough to make anyone start drinking. That soup should help. Give her our best, will you?"

"Sure thing." I tried to pay for the soup, but Silas wouldn't let me.

I waved goodbye to the women, but they had already taken their seats at a table, gossiping to the customers next to them. I wondered how much longer any of us could stand the Dramatic Duo staying in Clearview. This standoff wasn't doing anyone any good. If something didn't give soon, I didn't know what was going to happen.

I pulled into the drive of Chloe's cute little ranch. Her car was the only one there. The blinds were still closed. Maybe she was in bed. I rang the bell twice, but no one answered. I knocked, but still no answer. As a last-ditch effort, I pulled out a wipe and tried the doorknob.

The door swung open just as lightning streaked across the sky, a crack of thunder sounded, and the rain fell in a torrential downpour.

I rushed inside, shaking the water off my arms and closing the door behind me. "Chloe? It's Kalli Ballas."

"Kalli?" I heard Chloe call out in a shaky voice

from the kitchen. Something in her tone had my stomach dropping.

"I'm here. I brought you soup. Are you okay?"

"No, I'm not okay at all."

My heartbeat sped up. "I'm coming," I said as I walked toward the kitchen.

"H—hurry," she responded, sounding strange.

I came to a stop at the entrance of her kitchen, gasped, and promptly dropped the container of piping hot chicken soup. The container popped open and soup splattered everywhere. Covering my gaping mouth with my hands, my eyes shot to Chloe's. A mixture of shock, confusion and horror stared back at me. I forced my eyes to look at the floor one more time to confirm what my brain told me I had just seen.

Ariana Drakos lay lifelessly on Chloe Steven's kitchen floor with an empty bottle of Ouzo smashed over her head. I bent down with shaking hands and felt for a pulse on her neck. Nothing. Stepping back, I scrubbed my hands with hand sanitizer, feeling nauseous. Chloe looked at me, and I shook my head no. She rubbed her arms even though the summer heat was already stifling.

"What happened?" I asked when I could find my voice.

"I—I don't know." She stared at me with wide worried dark-brown eyes. "I don't remember anything between my third glass of Ouzo at midnight and waking up a half hour ago. What did I do?"

"Maybe nothing." I tried to reassure her though I had my own doubts. "Just know you're not in this alone." That much I could promise her. I liked Chloe, and Greek families stuck together.

I pulled out my phone and dialed a number I hadn't planned call ever again.

"Kalli, I'm so glad you called. I—" Nik's soft voice that had won me over from the start filled my insides with warmth, but I had to stay focused.

"You won't be when you hear why," I cut him off.

The line filled with a heavy silence. "What's wrong?" His suspicious tone was in full detective mode now.

"Ariana Drakos is dead."

"What?" Detective Stevens barked with authority. "Where are you?"

"Your ma's house."

He cursed, and the line went dead.

CLEARVIEW POLICE STATION was buzzing with activity. People had come from all over for the Precious Gems and Jewelry Fair held in our community center. Diehard gem collectors were crazy competitive when it came to dickering over jewelry. It didn't help matters that an early heat wave had settled over the town.

And now a dead body.

The last thing Clearview needed was a murder in the middle of the summer tourist season. Mayor Riboldazzi was breathing down Captain Crenshaw's neck to keep the peace and not let anything interfere with the fair, especially after a series of thefts had been happening at random businesses all over town for weeks now with no suspects. Half my relatives had been affected by the crimes and wanted answers.

I sat beside Chloe in the interrogation room. I had to give my statement. Besides, I'd promised I would be there for her. She hadn't told her family about the murder yet, but after half the emergency vehicles from the entire county had arrived at her house, I was sure they knew by now.

Nik had driven us to the police station and convinced his captain to let me stay for his mother's sake. They'd questioned Chloe for an hour but had gotten nowhere. I'd held her hand briefly and could confirm she really didn't remember what happened other than arguing with both Drakos women, then buying the Ouzo and having several glasses alone at home. She had no recollection of Ariana arriving or letting her in, but there was no sign of forced entry, so she must have.

"I know the whole town heard me say I hated Ariana, but I would never kill anyone, let alone a pregnant woman." Chloe made the sign of the cross and then wrung her hands in her lap. "I pray to the Gods you believe me, Nikos."

"Of course, I do, Ma." He might not love Ariana, but he had history with her and possibly a child. I couldn't imagine what emotions he was going through. "No one is saying you murdered her," he continued. "There's no proof of that, just circumstantial evidence." He knelt before his ma and took her hands in his own. "I'll find out what really happened. I can promise you that."

"I don't think it's a good idea for you to be on the investigation officially, Detective Stevens." Captain Crenshaw sat on the edge of the table with his arms crossed over his suit, studying both Nik and his mother.

"Why not?" Nik stood and faced him, his face set in a harsh frown. His sport coat had a stain on the lapel and his jeans were a wrinkled mess.

"You're too close to this case to be objective." Crenshaw's steel grey eyes locked onto Boomer's hazel ones. "Detective Matheson, I want you on this case."

Boomer shifted, his light-weight leather bomber jacket slung over his shoulder, his polo shirt tucked into his jeans. He didn't make eye contact with Nik when he responded. "You got it, Captain."

"Come on, Captain." Nik parted his sport coat and put his hands on his hips. "I can do this. Give me a shot."

Captain shook his head, his salt and pepper buzzcut not moving an inch. "I want you to stay on the series of thefts, Stevens."

"This is bull, Captain." Nik threw his hands in the air and began to pace. "Matheson can cover the Business Bandit just as well as I can."

"I don't want you anywhere near Ariana Drakos' murder case. She was your ex-girlfriend, possibly the mother of your child, and your own mother is the prime suspect. To say you have several conflicts of interest is putting it mildly." He stabbed his finger in Nik's direction. "If I catch you interfering, I'm hitting you with disciplinary action." Crenshaw locked eyes with Nik. "Am I clear?"

"Yes, sir," Nik ground out. "If there's nothing else, I would like to take my ma back to my place. She's been through enough for one day."

"You're dismissed, Detective. You know the drill." His gaze shot to Nik's mother. "Don't leave town, Ms. Stevens, and tell your relatives to do the same."

Chloe nodded as if in a daze.

"If you're finished with your statement, you're free to go, Ms. Ballas."

"Thank you, sir," I said and stood on shaky legs.

My gaze locked with Nik's as he helped his ma to her feet and took her arm. A world of unspoken emotions passed between us with a single glance, yet neither one of us seemed to know what to say or do about them, so we just stood there.

"Detective Matheson, can you give me a lift back to my car?" I finally asked.

"Sure," Boomer said.

That snapped Nik out of his stupor. He walked by me without looking at me then glared at Boomer without saying a word.

"Thank you," I replied, wondering if things would ever be the same between Nik and me. I didn't know the answer to that, but there was one thing I was certain of...

I was going to use my gift and offer up my two cents, for whatever it was worth.

CHAPTER 4

The next morning, I walked over to Nik's half of the house and knocked three times with my elbow. A loud thumping and whine started from behind the door. I bit back a smile.

Wolfgang.

There was a time I was terrified of the beast, but we had come to an understanding. Now, I couldn't help but find his unwavering love for me endearing.

"Wolfy, sit!" I heard Nik say.

Thump. Whine.

"I mean it, buddy. I'm not going to open this door until you behave."

Thump. Thump. Howl.

"Don't make me put you out back, because I will."

Thump. Thump. Thump. Bark!

"It's okay, Detective," I said.

All noise stopped.

"Are you sure?" he asked warily.

"I'm sure."

"Don't say I didn't warn you." He opened the door carefully, and Wolfgang's whine rose an octave when he spotted me. Every muscle in his huge body quivered as he sat back on his haunches, ready to pounce.

I thrust out my hand in a stay position and said firmly in my best no-nonsense tone, "Wolfgang Stevens, you sit your fanny down this instant!"

His fanny hit the floor with a loud flop, but didn't stop wiggling for a moment.

"Good boy," I said and carefully patted the top of his head.

His eyes rolled back in heaven, but he didn't dare move or he knew I would stop.

Nik ran a hand through his disheveled hair and shook his head. "I don't know how you do that."

I shrugged, then quickly pulled my hand away and scrubbed it with hand sanitizer. "It's our little secret." I cleared my throat. "May I come in?"

Nik masked his face of any emotion and stepped back to open the door wider. Wolfgang gave up and walked away, content for the moment, then circled before throwing his massive body down on a dog bed in the corner. The layout of Nik's half of the house was set up exactly the same as Jaz's and mine, but that's where the similarity ended. Jaz had put her stylish flair for decorating all over our side of the house. Modern elegance and class. Whereas the detective was a bachelor with a capital B. Bare minimum and nothing matched.

"How's Chloe?" I asked, following Nik into the living room.

He looked as if he'd been up all night with his wrinkled sweatpants and t-shirt, messy hair, and bare feet. He had dark circles beneath his eyes, and the lines on his forehead looked deeper, but he still smelled better than anything I could remember. Something uniquely him that was hard to ignore.

"She's in the kitchen. Doc LaLone gave her a sedative last night, but she refused to take it." He shoved his hands in his pockets. "She seems numb, and I don't know what to do. I hate feeling so helpless."

"I'm sure Detective Matheson is doing everything he can to figure this out."

"I'm not saying that Boomer's not a good detective, but this is my ma we're talking about. I can't just sit by and do nothing."

I pursed my brow. "What are you going to do? You don't want to mess this case up for your ma, or get yourself into trouble with the captain. Aren't you supposed to be investigating the recent string of thefts around town?"

"Yes, and I will, but you let me worry about my captain. If I happen to come across some useful piece of information regarding the murder while on the job, then you'd better believe I'll look into it. I've always been good at multi-tasking."

I care about Chloe too, so you can't get mad if I do the same, I thought, thankful he couldn't read *my* mind. He'd had a fit when I'd helped clear Jaz's name after she was accused of murder not that long ago.

He'd called it interfering.

I'd called it investigating.

It was my civic duty to keep my eyes and ears open; see something say something, and all that. This time was no exception, especially with the ace up my sleeve that no one except Jaz knew about.

"What?" He narrowed his eyes at me and pointed his finger in my face. "I know that look, Ballas. It spells trouble, and that's something my ma doesn't need any more of."

I brushed his finger aside and gave him a look that said, *I don't know what you're talking about*, and then asked, "Speaking of your ma, I brought her some herbal tea." I held up a bag and smiled a little too big. "Can I talk to her?"

"I don't think that's a good—"

"Nik, darling, is that Kalli I hear?"

"Yes, it's me, Chloe," I hollered back. "I brought you tea." I quickly stepped around the detective and made my way to the kitchen before he could stop me.

Chloe sat at the kitchen table, looking far more put together than her son. She wore a pair of white dress shorts with a peach blouse. Her hair was perfectly styled and makeup flawless. Her bloodshot eyes were the only indication that she'd just been through a traumatic event the day before.

I went straight to the cupboard and pulled down two mugs, then put the kettle on, making myself right at home. Nik had bought the kettle just for me because he knew how much I liked tea, and had even started keeping a container of wipes on the counter. He came in grudgingly and poured a cup of coffee, spooning a teaspoon of something into it, then sat at the table next to his ma with a pout on his handsome face. Nikos clearly didn't like losing, that was for sure.

A moment later, I turned the kettle off and poured hot water over our tea, then brought the mugs to the table.

"Thank you, dear. This is so kind of you." Chloe bobbed her tea bag in the mug while it steeped.

"You're very welcome, Chloe." I turned my gaze on Nik. "Did you use pure sugar in your coffee?" I asked him.

He arched one eyebrow high in answer.

"Because artificial sweeteners rot your insides and may cause irritable bowel syndrome." I took a sip of my black tea.

"I'll keep that in mind," he said dryly.

I shrugged. "Don't say I didn't warn you if, you know, something strange starts going on with your digestive system."

He ignored me and focused on his ma. His eyes widened as he stared at her neck, then he frowned. "How come you're wearing the family heirloom, Ma?"

Her fingertips fluttered and touched the pendent attached to a gold chain around her neck as if she just remembered she had it on. She sighed sadly, shaking her head as if still stunned over everything that had happened. "I usually only wear it on special occasions, but I figured it couldn't hurt to wear it now."

"It's been in our family forever, Ma. You always told me no one should wear it. What if you lose it? You really shouldn't wear it at all, especially not to any more Sunday brunches. What if you lose it, and your lawn service mows over it?"

She stuck her chin out. "I know what I said, but it makes me feel good."

"What's the point of jewelry if you can't wear it? I say go for it." I took a sip of tea, ignoring the evil eye directed at me from across the table. I was here to help; my methods were just different than his. "I still don't understand why Ariana was at your house that late at night. My YiaYia always says nothing good happens after midnight."

"Apparently, your grandma is right," Chloe said.

Nikos grunted.

"I can't imagine why Ariana paid me a visit then, either," Chloe went on. "Although it doesn't really surprise me. The girl was relentless in her pursuit of my son. Unfortunately, I don't remember a thing." She sipped her tea and looked off as if working something out in her head. "It's strange because I've had more

Ouzo in the past than I did that night and never woke up not remembering anything."

"Do you think someone could have drugged you?" I asked, trying to make sense of it all. She hadn't gone to a bar or anything. She'd gone to the grocery store, the liquor store, and then home, according to the rumor mill.

"Already thought of that," Nik chimed in, back to his detective self. "Detective Matheson is having the bottle of Ouzo analyzed, though why someone would want to drug my ma is a mystery."

"No more mystery than why someone would want to kill Ariana," Chloe added. "I just don't understand what's going on."

"Maybe we can start there," I said. "Come up with a list of people who might have wanted to see Ariana dead. Or people who had a grudge against her ma. Someone who might want to get back at her by killing her only child."

Chloe barked out a harsh laugh. "Get in line. Those two made their fair share of enemies back in the city and already here in Clearview."

"We?" Nik asked. "There is no *we*, Kalli. If I'm not allowed on this case, you sure as hell aren't."

"Nikos, language, please. Last time I checked, I was your mama. I'm the one whose name needs clearing. I have a say in whose help I want," his ma added firmly. "I say the more the merrier because it looks like I can use all the help I can get."

"This is crazy, Ma. Kalli isn't—" His cell phone rang. He glanced at the caller ID. "I have to take this." He walked away. "What's up, Matheson?" My Dreamy Detective paced. "Interesting." He turned around and paced the other way and then stopped abruptly.

"You're sure?" He listened. "There's no mistake?" His jaw hardened. "Thanks for the update. Keep me posted if you hear anything else."

"What is it?" his ma asked.

"What's wrong?" I asked at the same time.

He blew out a breath before answering. "The bottle of Ouzo was laced with a benzodiazepine called Flurazepam, used for insomnia. It's pretty strong. That's why you didn't wake up."

"I knew I didn't have too much to drink." Chloe slapped the table before her. "But why would someone do that to me?"

"They found an open bottle in your medicine cabinet, Ma. There's no proof someone did that to you."

"Well, that's ridiculous. I'm not the best sleeper. I mean, who is at my age. But I certainly have never taken sleeping pills, especially with alcohol. Your Uncle Ramos never woke up after mixing the two." She made the sign of the cross. "Why do you think I didn't take the sedative Doc LaLone gave me yesterday?"

"I believe you, Ma. It just doesn't look good." He pinched the bridge of his nose. "That's not all Detective Matheson had to say."

We both snapped our heads in Nik's direction.

"I wasn't the father of Ariana's baby."

My heart flipped.

Chloe gasped.

"I don't get it. How can you tell who the father is this early?" I asked.

"Because Ariana lied." His gaze met mine, full of regret and longing to reverse this setback in our relationship as he finished with, "She was never pregnant in the first place."

"I'll kill her." Chloe slammed her fist on the table then stood up.

"She's already dead, Ma, and the police think you killed her because of comments like that." He motioned for her to sit back down.

She complied, looking defeated as she said, "Oh, woe is me," and made the sign of the cross again.

"Why would Ariana try to trap you with a baby if she wasn't actually pregnant? She had to know you would eventually find out." My mind was whirling, trying to sort out all the possibilities, but nothing was making sense.

"I have no clue." Nik's face filled with anger and determination as he added, "but I'm not going to rest until I find out."

~

That afternoon, I took Chloe to Hera's Halo. Aunt Tasoula said my ma stole the goddess of love and beauty, Aphrodite, for her restaurant name, so Tasoula chose the queen of the gods, Hera, for her hair salon. The sisters loved each other, but that didn't stop their competitive spirits from trying to outdo each other every chance they got.

Detective Stevens was in no mood to listen to his ma or me speculate on the case, probably because the artificial sweetener had kicked in. I'd told him as much, but he said I was nuts. Then he rushed off because another theft had occurred. This time at Vixen, a high-end clothing store owned by Jaz's competition, Anastasia Stewart.

Jaz and Ana weren't exactly friends, but she could relate to how Ana must feel because her shop had been hit a couple weeks ago by the Business Bandit. It was also apparent this thief was a pro. Nik had his work cut out for him, which was why he needed me more than ever, even if he didn't know it.

"Thank you so much, Kalli," Chloe said as we sat in the waiting room of the salon.

"Of course." I placed a handkerchief I kept in my purse on the seat and sat down beside her. "My aunt has been begging me to come in and let her work her magic since I got home from the city."

"Aunt Tasoula knows best." My aunt winked, and Ma grunted.

Chloe picked up a magazine of celebrity gossip news to thumb through, then sat in a chair. The chairs looked like gold thrones, the capes like a queen's robe, and even the dryers were painted like crowns with precious gems adorning them. "I'm going stir crazy staying at my son's house. He won't let me make a move."

"That's not good for the circulation, you know. You're going to get the clot," my ma said on a shiver as she sat under the dryer.

"My cousin Nefeli got the clot, and it went straight to her brain, God rest her soul," My Aunt Tasoula said as she cut Nik's cousin Thalia's hair.

The waiting room full of Greek women made the sign of the cross.

"You mean a blood clot?" I asked, amazed over the way my family's brains worked. Maybe if I were full Greek, I would understand them. Every time I thought I'd seen and heard it all, they still managed to surprise me.

"I don't know what the clot is made out of, I just know it's no good." Aunt Tasoula tsked as she snipped away.

"This whole situation isn't good," Thalia said. "And

it's certainly not fair." Her dark brown eyes hardened, and her tone filled with disgust. "I hate to speak ill of the dead, but Ariana Drakos was *not* a good person."

"What do you mean?" I walked over to the beverage counter behind Thalia and poured myself a glass of cucumber water so I could hear every word.

"I'm a realtor back in the city. I spent years building my reputation and growing my client list. Ariana never liked me. She only became a realtor because I was one, then she slept with half my clients just to steal them out from under me."

"Benny Balboa was your client before he started dating Ariana, wasn't he?" Chloe lowered her magazine and looked at Thalia in question.

"He sure was, and not only that, Benny liked me first. We had just started going on dates when she came along and ruined things."

"Consider yourself lucky." Chloe scoffed. "He's connected to the mob. When Nikos found that out, he dumped her."

"What I don't understand is why come back and lie to Nik about being pregnant if she was with Benny again?" Thalia threw that little tidbit out there.

We had just found out there was never a baby, yet the beauty of a small town was the word had already gotten around. My lips tipped down. More importantly, Thalia's words registered.

"Wait, what makes you think Ariana was with Benny again?" I asked.

"I saw them huddled close, talking together outside the Precious Gems and Jewelry Fair. What else would he be doing in Clearview? It was bad enough when she messed with my life, but I'm not about to stand by and let her mess with my family's. Nikos didn't deserve to be her pawn in whatever twisted game she was playing. I was going to tell him what I saw, but fate intervened and now I don't have to."

I stumbled and dropped my glass of water over her words, glass shattering and water flying everywhere, as I grabbed her shoulder to steady myself. *I also saw the manipulating monster sneak into Aunt Chloe's House. As far as I'm concerned, she got what she deserved, and I'm not one bit sorry for thinking that.*

"Oh, dear, are you okay?" Aunt Tasoula went to grab my arm.

I quickly stepped back and wiped my hands on my skirt. "Sorry, Aunt Tasoula. Clumsy me. I'll clean that up."

"Don't be silly. That's what I pay my grandson Christos the big bucks for." She looked at the fourteen-year-old and he stared at her blankly. She made a mopping motion. He rolled his eyes, put down his phone, then went in the back to grab the bucket. "This generation, they never want to work," she said loud enough for him to hear.

"I'm really sorry," I said to Thalia. "I hope I didn't hurt you."

"Don't worry about me. I'm fine." She rubbed her shoulder from my death grip then looked in the mirror and her eyes widened.

"What?" My aunt waved her scissors about as she talked. "You be fine. Short hair suits you better anyway. You'll see."

The only thing I could see were new clues and unanswered questions. What was Benny Balboa doing in town with Ariana? Why would Ariana pretend to be pregnant with Nik's child? What was Thalia Pagonis doing in the middle of the night to see Ariana sneaking into Chloe Stevens house? What else had she seen? Why didn't she tell the police?

I might not be a detective, but that didn't mean I couldn't be of help. At least now I had direction on where to start.

CHAPTER 5

An hour later, Nik walked into my aunt's hair salon, and his eyes widened when he took one look at me. Aunt Tasoula claimed that, at her salon, she could make anyone look like an angel. More like a member of the biker gang, Hell's Angels. I loved the woman dearly, but our tastes were definitely not the same.

She was just unsnapping the special cape she'd wrapped around me. She knew I would never wear the capes she draped around everyone else, no matter how well she sanitized them. So, she kept a special pink one just for me that no one else was allowed to touch, and cleaned the chair thoroughly before I sat down, of course. She'd tried to give me highlights, but I drew the line at that. Good lord, who knew what ingredients were in the colors she bought. I, however, compromised and let her trim my split ends and style my locks.

Big mistake.

I had chills that were multiplying all right, and I was terrified of what that was doing to my nerve endings. She'd teased my hair twice as high as any beauty school dropout, except she hadn't dropped out of anything and was the only cosmetologist in town.

"I could have given your ma a ride home, Detective," I said, hoping to ward off any comments about my hair.

"Nice to see you, too, Ms. Ballas," he said dryly.

"Sorry. Hi, Nik." I inhaled deeply and tried to relax. I needed to find a way to dissolve the tension between us, so he would let down his guard. I knew he would never let me help with the investigation, but I also knew he needed my help. I would do anything to help his ma. "Friends?" I held out my hand.

He wrapped his palm around mine, and I felt the electricity straight through my core. *Why did I have to mess up? Man up. Take what you can get and work on the rest. Prove you're worthy of a second chance.* He stared deep into my eyes with his intense, piercing blue gaze and flashed a smile that sucker punched my gut. "Sure. Friends." *For now.*

I pulled my hand from his and rubbed my palm on my skirt, which only made his smile turn tender and endearing.

"New look?" His lips quirked as his gaze took in my bee's nest.

"*Temporary* look." I shuddered, patting my poufy head. "But seriously, how come you're here."

"I texted him about what Thalia said." Chloe had joined us with a fresh hairdo herself, still looking picture perfect in every way. "I worry my niece may have done something stupid. She and Ariana have never gotten along. She won't admit it, but we all knew she had a serious thing for Benny, like more than a fling. Ariana stealing him was the last straw."

"I had no idea he was in town." Nik's jaw hardened.

"Thalia is still here if you want to talk to her. I saw her go in the back." Chloe pointed to the far corner of the room.

Nik headed in that direction, and I followed. He stopped in his tracks, and I bumped into him. "Where are you going?"

"With you." I straightened my blouse. He narrowed his eyes, and I shrugged. "My purse is in the back." Thank goodness I'd put it there when I'd grabbed my special cape, but I would have followed him regardless.

We heard the back door open and both hurried forward, no time left to argue, thank the lord.

"Thalia, wait up," Nik hollered as we walked out the back door just before Thalia could get in her car.

The sun was already high in the sky. It was going to be another scorcher. I shaded my eyes and followed him closely.

Thalia was tall and willowy slim with a new bobbed haircut after Aunt Tasoula's mishap with the scissors. I had to admit the haircut was flattering on her. How come everyone else's hair looked fabulous while I looked like a troll doll?

"Hey, Nikos, it's so good to see you. I feel like we haven't had two seconds to catch up." Thalia gave him a hug then eyed me curiously over his shoulder.

I waved but didn't say anything. I was discovering it was often better to listen and observe.

"It's good to see you, too, cuz." Nik let go of her, and his expression changed to one of concern. "What's going on, Thalia? Ma told me what you said in the salon."

Her face flushed pink. "What do you mean? It's all true."

"You mean to tell me Benny Balboa is in town?"

She nodded. "I saw him the day after Ariana and her mother ruined your ma's brunch with her ridiculous accusations that weren't even true."

"He could just be in town for the Precious Gems and Jewelry Fair." Nik's face registered distaste. "He always did have a thing for lots of bling."

Thalia was already shaking her head. "I saw them huddled together with their heads close in conversation outside the community center. They looked pretty chummy to me. For someone who was supposedly pregnant with your child, who wanted to marry you, why was she talking to her ex?"

"Is that why you spied on them when you saw Ariana sneak into Chloe's house the night of the murder?" I asked.

Her eyes widened as they settled on me. "How did you know?"

Well, shoot. I kept forgetting what was said out loud versus what I had heard when I read people's minds. "You said it when you were getting your hair cut. Don't you remember?" I pasted on the most innocent confused expression.

Her forehead creased. "I seriously don't remember saying that."

Nik gave me a funny look before studying his cousin. "It doesn't matter when you said it. Kalli obviously heard you, so you must have. Come on, Thalia, tell us everything you know. This is Ma we're talking about."

"I knew Ariana was up to no good, Nikky. I couldn't let her trap you, so I followed her. I thought for sure that she would meet up with Benny, but I was surprised when she went to your ma's house."

"Did you see anyone else at Ma's house that night?"

"I'm sorry, no. Once I realized Benny wasn't there, I left. I wish I would have stayed longer to see if anyone else showed up. It looked like your ma had let her in because Ariana literally walked right in. I thought the door must have been unlocked, almost as if your ma had been expecting her. It seemed odd that Aunt Chloe would be having company that late at night, but as long as Ariana wasn't with Benny, I figured it was none of my business, so I went home."

"Ma said she opened the bottle to let it breathe while she changed into her pajamas, then took the bottle to bed with her and didn't hear anything until morning." Nik studied her carefully. "Did you know the bottle of Ouzo was laced with a sleep aid? Ma doesn't ever take sleep aids, so someone drugged her."

Thalia's mouth fell open. "You seriously don't think that someone was me, do you?" Her eyes filled with tears.

A lengthy pause filled the air before he blew out a sigh. "Of course, I believe you, but I'm not the one in charge of the investigation. Detective Matheson is."

"You're not going to tell him, are you?"

"You already told the whole room, Thalia." Nik opened his sport coat and rested his hands on his jean clad hips.

Technically she hadn't told the whole room everything, but the info was out now and my lips were sealed.

"Clearview is a small town," he went on. "Detective Matheson is a good detective. He's going to find out."

I reached out and squeezed her shoulder. She

blinked at me as if just remembering I was still there and had heard everything. *Oh no, what have I done? I have to find a way out of this mess.* I heard her think. I dropped my hand in confusion.

What the heck did that mean?

LATER THAT EVENING, I went to Full Disclosure to get some work done. I was up in the loft, sketching a fall collection of Kalli Original lingerie designs since my spring and summer lines were already out. My head was still swirling over everything I'd heard that afternoon at the salon.

"Hey, girl. I'm starving. What do you feel like for dinner?" Jaz asked when she reached the top of the stairs. She used the hand sanitizer I kept at the top of the stairs but didn't go any further than that, knowing I liked my space to be a safety zone from germs, and I loved her for it.

I had filled Jaz in on the afternoon events when I'd first arrived at the boutique, then the store became busy, so we hadn't talked since.

"I'm not hungry so order whatever you feel like."

"Okay." She didn't make a move to leave, finally saying, "I still can't believe Ariana was never pregnant. I mean, who does that? Why try to totally disrupt someone's life when you know they're going to eventually find out. It doesn't make any sense."

"I know, right?" I shook my fuller-than-normal hair, even after three shampoos. "I just don't get why on earth she was conspiring with her ex-boyfriend if she was trying to win Nik over?"

"Exactly." Jaz slapped her hand on the banister.

"She had to have some ulterior motive, but we'll never know now that she's deceased."

"Unless we find the ex-boyfriend. I'd bet my last bottle of hand sanitizer he knows something."

"I'd wager you're right. And I love how you said *we*." Her amber eyes twinkled with excitement and mischief. "You know I'll help you with anything you ever need. All you have to do is ask."

"I know you would. And I appreciate that so much, but I don't want to put you in a funny situation now that your boyfriend is the lead detective on this case."

"Oh, please." She waved her hand in the air. "You let me worry about my boyfriend." She studied me carefully. "Speaking of boyfriends. Now that you know there was no baby, are you going to give Detective Dreamy a second chance?"

"I don't know. His life is still so complicated, and with his ma the prime suspect in a murder investigation, it's not the time or the place to even think about romance."

"Did you at least tell him about your gift?"

I started shaking my head. "That would be a hard no. He already thinks I'm a little nutty. I don't want to turn him off completely."

"Quirky, not nutty." She smiled in such a genuine way, full of love and acceptance like only a best friend could do, always making me feel normal instead of freaky. "There's a difference, you know."

"If you say so then it must be true."

"I do." She blew me a kiss.

"Well, thank you. Anyway, speaking of gifts. I plan to use mine to help clear Chloe's name."

"I figured as much, even though Captain Crenshaw specifically told you both to steer clear." Jaz shook her head at me but then laughed. "Honestly, if it were Boomer's mother, I'd be doing the same. And I know for certain he would never butt out. In fact, I'm surprised Nik is staying out of the investigation."

"He's not. That's why he needs my help before he gets all of us in trouble and makes the situation worse for his ma. I'm still not sure Nik's cousin, Thalia, isn't hiding something. And I need to find out where Benny is staying and why he is in town."

"I probably shouldn't be saying anything, but well, you're my best friend. So, Boomer let it slip during pillow talk that he was looking into Ariana's possible enemies. I guess both she and her mother made some enemies during their short time in town. For example, Nelson Rockwell of Rockwell Jewelers was none too pleased with Ariana. She tried to pawn her jewelry off on him. Turns out they were fakes. Shortly after that, some of his genuine jewelry went missing. He blamed her, but she claimed he was crazy, and he vowed to get back at her. Several people witnessed the incident, including Milly Donovan, the local dog walker who walks past his shop every day."

"Interesting."

"What's interesting?" Detective Matheson appeared at the top of the stairs behind Jaz and kissed her cheek. He knew not to cross the invisible line into my sanctuary as well.

Jaz shot me a warning look.

"Oh, nothing really. I was asking Jaz if she knew a good jeweler."

He studied me with his intelligent hazel eyes. "Why? You wouldn't be sticking your nose in where it didn't belong, would you? Because it's not just Captain Crenshaw who wants Detective Stevens to stay out of this case. Mayor Riboldazzi wants the case closed asap, before it ruins the summer tourist season."

"I'm not Detective Stevens." I crossed my arms over my chest.

"No, but last I checked, you were guilty by association."

"Relax, Big Guy. That association is no more." I grabbed my satchel full of fabric samples, pins, and my sketchbook and stuffed all the supplies I'd draped over my mannequin inside. "Nik's ma has an heirloom necklace she wants to get appraised. I'm just trying to help." She'd never actually said that, but maybe she should have. Either way, it gave me the excuse I needed.

"Really, he never mentioned it to me."

"He's busy investigating the Business Bandit, remember? Besides, it's a girl thing. Something you detectives don't need to worry about. I've got it covered." I winked. "You worry about the case, and I'll worry about Nik's ma."

"Where are you going?" Jaz gave me a worried look.

"I'm fine, just tired. I'm going to head home."

"Are you sure you're not hungry?"

"I brought your favorite sushi to surprise you," Boomer said to Jaz and held up a bag he'd had hidden behind his back. "There's plenty here."

Jaz's whole face softened. "Oh, that's so sweet, Babe." Then she chewed her bottom lip and looked at me. "Want to share?"

"I promise, I'm okay, but thank you. I'll grab something light at home. You two kids have fun." I smiled a sincere smile, truly happy for her. "Besides, I have to feed Prissy. You know how the princess fusses if I make her wait too long to eat."

"Okay. Hey, before I forget to ask you, do you want to go to the Precious Gems and Jewelry Fair tomorrow? I haven't had a chance yet to go, and I'm dying to check it out. I heard this year there are some amazing finds."

"Sure thing. We'll figure out a time later," I said as I waited for them to walk down the stairs. I followed at a safe distance behind, reminding myself to clean the railing tomorrow after the Fair. The community center had been the next place I'd wanted to investigate, and my best friend had just given me a reason to go.

CHAPTER 6

The next morning, Jaz and I arrived at the community center. You would never know a murder had taken place recently in our small town. The Precious Gems and Jewelry Fair was packed. Collectors were serious about competing for the best finds. After circling the parking lot of the community center for ten minutes, we finally found a spot.

We made our way inside the building, and the air conditioning blasted us, terrifying me when I thought about the filtration system. I would rather deal with the heat than the germs I was undoubtedly breathing in, but I didn't have a choice. I needed answers and had to follow where the clues led me, no matter the cost to my health and sanity. I tried to focus on more pleasant things. Fluorescent lights bathed all the booths, making the stones sparkle. New age music filtered through the sound system, mixing with the hum of conversation.

"Of course, Mrs. Flannigan is here." Jaz pointed across the room. "That women will never pass up the opportunity for a sale."

Michael Flannigan owned the local Irish pub and

was always working. They'd never been blessed with children, so he let his wife Lois shop for anything she wanted to keep her happy. She was a regular at Jaz's shop and always had the latest scoop on hot ticket items around town. She was talking animatedly with Eleanor and Olivia Bennett, no doubt informing them which displays were the best.

"Let's go say hi." I felt plain, dressed in my cotton shorts and t-shirt. It was hard going anyplace with my best friend, the fashion icon. She didn't try to make anyone feel out of place, she was just naturally stunning. It was like constantly walking around with a super model.

"Good call. Between the three of them, we'll get the best deal and advice on which stones best suit us." Jaz rubbed her hands together, looking fresh and trendy in a pleated skort and collared shirt with the sleeves rolled up.

"Well, hello, ladies." Lois beamed, the rosy cheeks on each side of her smile matching her hair. She was clearly in her element. "You're in luck. Today, a few booths are giving fifty percent off. Isn't that the cat's meow?" She clapped.

"That's fabulous." Jaz looked around in awe like Alice in Wonderland.

"Oh, honey, you should really visit the emerald booth. Those stones would match your eyes perfectly," Eleanor said to me.

"Thank you for the tip. I'll keep that in mind."

Olivia's gaze traveled over my head. "Did you do something different to your hair, dear? It looks extra, um, *full* today."

"Oh, something like that. My Aunt Tasoula loves to pump up the volume." I patted my head to no avail. The strands sprung right back up.

"She certainly does." Jaz chuckled. "Okay, so what about me, ladies?" Jaz twirled around in a circle. "What do you think would look good on me?"

"Anything," they both said in unison and then laughed.

"They're right," Lois chimed in, then added, "and if you don't find anything you like here, you should visit Nelson's Rockwell's store."

"Oh, he has some fantastic pieces there," Eleanor agreed. "Some of his items are one-of-a-kind. You can't find them anyplace else."

"Good idea. Chloe Stevens wanted me to take her there to have a family heirloom necklace appraised anyway."

"Well, he's certainly the right man for that job. I think he's here if you want to talk to him." Olivia looked around. "Ah, yes, there he is. Over in the corner by that man." She pointed and then paused before adding, "Oh, my. I'm not sure I would try to talk to him now, though. They don't look too happy."

Jaz and I glanced at each other and then over to the corner. Nelson was a Ken doll replica in his forties, with lacquered light brown hair parted on the side. He had his arms folded across his chest and his spine ramrod straight. His jaw was clenched and lips pressed together in a firm line, while a younger, beefier man yelled at him with his finger thrust in his face. The man had a buzzcut, a chiseled jaw, and a deep dimple in his chin.

"Who is that?" I asked.

"I have no clue." Jaz studied the man. "I'm not sure I've ever seen him before. Whoever he is, they definitely don't like each other."

"I saw him right here at the community center on the first day of the Fair." Lois looked around then leaned in closer to us. "He was with that girl who got murdered. Until her mother caught them, that is. She let him have it before hauling her daughter, the floosy, away. Poor Detective Stevens."

Eleanor snapped her finger. "I know who he is. I remember him coming into Rockwell Jewelers when sister and I were shopping."

"That's right." Olivia nodded. "I'm pretty sure he said his name was Benny something. He was showing some jewelry to Nelson."

Benny Balboa.

Things just kept getting more and more interesting. What in the world could Ariana Drakos' ex want with Nelson Rockwell? A noise and raised voices broke through my thoughts and I looked back over to the corner.

Benny shoved Nelson hard and then headed for the nearest exit.

"Hey, I'm gonna step out for some air. You coming?" I gave Jaz a look and jerked my head in the direction of Benny.

Jaz's eyes widened, and then she winked. "I don't think so. I'd like these lovely ladies to help me pick something out over at the amber table. I'll catch up with you later." She steered the busybodies in the other direction.

Not wasting another minute, I made a beeline for the far corner door. I wasn't paying attention to my surroundings and bounced off the chest of a very large bald man. He looked down at me with surprise. "Careful, there," he said with the deepest voice I'd ever heard. "Wouldn't want to see you get hurt."

"Thanks. Sorry about that. Enjoy the Fair." I hurried around him, feeling his eyes watch me as I walked away.

Moments later, I stepped out the door and searched the area. I didn't see anything. Disappointment streaked through me at the missed opportunity. The door I'd exited led to the back parking lot of the community center where delivery trucks entered. I missed a step, seeing a germy dumpster before me. Spinning my fidget ring, I held my breath and peered behind my worst nightmare and along the edge of the trees.

"Looking for me?" came a husky voice from behind me.

I jumped and stumbled as I turned around.

Strong hands reached out and grabbed my arms to steady me. *Wow, you're a looker, sweetheart. You want me, you got me.*

"I don't think so," I said, pulling my arms away and trying not to shiver despite the heat. A dangerous vibe oozed out of his very pores, making me second-guess my decision to confront him alone. His ex-girlfriend or still-girlfriend or whatever she was to him had just been murdered. He certainly hadn't wasted any time in moving on. I fished my handy dandy bottle out of my short's pocket and sanitized my hands.

His lips hardened into a flat line.

"I mean, I wasn't looking for anyone. It's so dirty in there, and stuffy." I shoved the bottle back into my shorts. "I needed to get some air." I twisted my hair into a knot and wrapped the hairband from my wrist around the strands to secure them in place.

"I saw you staring at me from across the room, and then you just happen to wander out the same door as me and look around suspiciously." He studied me with stormy gray eyes. "I know when I'm being followed, lady."

"Okay, you caught me." I ran my fingertips behind my ear and down my neck to discreetly check my pulse. It was beating at an alarming rate and not because the man was attractive, which he was in a dark and scary way, but that was beside the point. He was huge and intimidating and linked to the mob.

His gaze tracked my finger and lingered. He took a step closer, and I quickly dropped my hand.

"Mind telling my why you were looking for me?" He brushed a strand of my hair that had escaped my messy bun behind my ear, and I grabbed his hand and held on tight, ignoring my urge to find a bar of soap. *Now you're talking, Darlin'. Stevens sure does have good taste, but I plan to get what I deserve. Just like I did before when I—*

I sucked in a sharp breath when Benny jerked out of my grip, but I was even more surprised he knew who I was. That couldn't be a good sign.

"Don't you dare touch her, Balboa," Detective Stevens ground out, his fists balled by his sides as if he struggled not to get violent.

I twisted my hands together three times as I watched them. I had to admit I'd been nervous around Benny, but I don't think he would have hurt me in broad daylight. Although, we were out back and no one was around. Still, Nik had terrible timing. If only he'd given me one more minute, I might have heard what Benny had done.

"What are you going to do about it, Detective? I can touch whoever I want." He looked at me. "Are you two a couple?"

My gaze shot to Nik's, and his jaw hardened, but he didn't say anything. He was waiting for me, but I wasn't ready to declare us anything. Besides, I didn't want to close the door on getting more information out of Benny. So, I looked back at him and shook my head no ever so slightly.

"Well, there you have it. Not that it would have made a difference when it comes to you and me," he said to Nik. "I take what I want." His lips curled into a sneer.

Nik cursed and lunged at Benny with fists raised just as Detective Matheson came around the corner.

"What's going on here," Boomer said, grabbing Nik just in time. "Jaz called me, and I'm glad she did by the look of it."

"I didn't do a thing." Benny held his hands up, his expression one of confused innocence until he looked at me and winked.

My stomach turned sour.

Nik jerked out of Boomer's grip and walked several steps away before returning. "Nothing's going on. I thought Balboa was bothering Ms. Ballas, but apparently I was wrong." He wouldn't look at me.

"Was Mr. Balboa bothering you, Ms. Ballas?" Detective Matheson stared at me, waiting for my reply.

"I'm sorry. This has all been one big mix-up. I came out here for some air. I don't like crowds." I fanned my face, not lying about that at least. "I didn't realize Mr. Balboa was out here. He wasn't bothering me. He just thought I had come out to see him. No harm done. Can we all leave now?"

"You two can," Boomer said as he studied Benny. "I have some questions I'd like to ask Mr. Balboa. We can either do it here, or we can go down to the station. What's it going to be, Benny?"

"We can go to the station. I have nothing to hide." He looked at Nik. "But I don't want him anywhere near me."

"Oh, don't worry." Boomer glared hard at Nik. "Detective Stevens has other matters to look into. He isn't on this case. Right, Stevens?"

A muscle in Nik's jaw pulsed before he nodded once and then walked away.

My heart sank as it felt like he was walking away from more than this case. I'd disappointed him. I could tell. But I had an idea on how to make it up to him.

~

THAT EVENING, I knocked on Nik's door. The sun was just beginning to set, painting the cloudless sky pink, purple, and orange, and a balmy breeze caressed my face. Jaz had taken Chloe out for dinner to take her mind off the case, and as a favor to me. I'd spent hours making Nik's favorite dinner, according to his ma. Now I just had to get him to agree to it, seeing as how he hadn't answered my calls or text messages all day.

Chloe said he'd been working on the Business Bandit case but had been home for an hour. She'd said he looked exhausted. He'd taken a shower and was now pouring over his notes on his ma's case, determined to investigate on his own time. She was worried about him, and so was I.

Even I knew we needed to talk. We needed a truce, and we needed to work together if we were going to be of any help to his ma. So, I knocked again.

Finally, the door opened.

He stood there in athletic shorts, a tank top, and bare feet. His skin was even more tan than his normal olive complexion, making his blue eyes even more piercing. His five o'clock shadow was thicker than normal, giving him an extra rugged appeal. He ran a hand through his messy dark brown curls and glanced at the yoga pants and tank top that I'd changed into after doing some sketching.

I swallowed hard, putting one bare foot on top of the other, trying not to squirm under his scrutiny as I reminded myself why dating him right now would be a bad idea. How was it that he always smelled amazing?

"Kalli, what are you doing here?" He sounded tired, yet his honey smooth voice was still hypnotic.

I shook out of my trance. "I have a surprise for you."

"I honestly don't think I can handle any more surprises."

"Just come with me." I grabbed his hand. *Why? There's nothing left to say between us.* "Yes, there is."

"Yes, there is what?" His brow puckered.

"I mean, yes, you can. Handle another surprise, that is." I had to remember he didn't know I could hear his thoughts.

He sighed, but let me drag him into my half of the house. *If you don't want to date me, you seriously have to stop letting your hair down and wearing pants that make your b—*

I dropped his hand and quickly turned around to face him.

"Are you okay?" He frowned, lifting a hand to feel my forehead. "Your cheeks are flushed, and you look out of breath."

I jumped back before he could touch me. "Hot flash," I said, which made no sense given my age. So, I pointed to my dining room table and changed the subject. "Ta-da. Your favorite dinner. Tzatziki chicken and spanakopita pinwheels with spinach and feta cheese. I only hope it's as good as your ma's."

His eyes widened when he looked at the perfectly

set table, with food steaming hot and ready to eat. His voice softened, and eyes filled with tenderness and wonder as they met mine once more. "You did this for me?"

I couldn't afford to love the way he looked at me sometimes, so I shrugged and walked past him to the table. "You've got to eat, right?" I gestured for him to sit. "Besides, I owe you an apology."

"No, you don't. I get it. I asked you out on a date, and then my ex-girlfriend showed up claiming to be pregnant with my baby. That's a lot for anyone to take on. Then she's murdered and we find out there was never any baby to begin with, not to mention her ex-mob boyfriend was in town with her. I have no idea why or what they could possibly have been up to." He stared down at his plate. "Even I wouldn't want to date me."

"Still," I responded softly. "I didn't have to say no in front of Benny."

He raised his head. "It was the truth. I didn't expect you to lie to save my ego. I was just jealous, but I got over it." He looked me in the eye. "Truce?"

"Yes, and more. Friends?"

"Absolutely." He smiled and looked sincere.

It's what I wanted, I told myself, but couldn't help feeling a little disappointed when he agreed so easily.

"Great." I forced a wide smile. "Let's celebrate." I opened a bottle of pinot grigio wine, poured two glasses, and took a healthy sip. "Now that we're buddy-buddy, maybe we should work together for the sake of your ma."

"What do you mean?" His eyes narrowed as he took a sip of wine as well. "Is that the real reason for this dinner?"

"Oh, come on. We both know neither one of us is

going to sit idly by while Detective Matheson investigates. And no, I meant my apology."

"Kalli, us working together is not a good idea." He dug into his food as if the matter was solved.

"Sure, it is. You know Boomer isn't going to tell you anything because he's by the book when it comes to Captain Crenshaw. But Jaz can't help herself. She lets things slip all the time to me without even realizing it."

"You've got a point." He studied me while he chewed, then pointed his fork in my direction. "But I know how you are. I don't want you putting yourself in danger."

"That's why it would be a good idea to *unofficially* work together." I took a mouthful of food myself, playing the game right along with him.

"I don't know about this." He took another sip of wine, pondering.

"Put it this way. You know I'm going to follow any lead I get on my own anyway, so why not ease your mind and come with me." I fluttered my eyelashes at him and held my hands clasped in front of me.

"You've definitely got a point there." He set his fork down on a sigh. "Okay, tell me what you've got."

"Well, Jaz told me Boomer said Ariana tried to pawn her fake jewelry off on Nelson Rockwell. Then Milly Donovan, the dog walker, witnessed him blaming Ariana when some of his jewelry went missing. He vowed to get back at her."

"That much I know because he called me after the robbery. He thought Ariana was the Business Bandit, but we've had more thefts since her murder, so she couldn't be."

"Maybe she was half the Bandit, and Benny was her sidekick. Jaz and I ran into Lois Flannigan, and she said she saw him at the Precious Gems and Jewelry Fair at the community center on the first day. Then the Bennett sisters said they saw him at the Rockwell's Jewelry Store before the murder as well. Then Jaz and I witnessed Nelson and Benny in a heated argument at the community center while we were there. That's the real reason why I followed Benny outside. I wanted to question him about why they were arguing. Nelson left before I had a chance to talk to him."

"I'll follow up with Nelson about the jewelry theft and see if I can get anything out of him about Benny." Nik grabbed a pen and pad of paper from a nearby table and jotted down some notes.

Suddenly, my phone rang. I checked the caller ID, and my stomach flipped.

"Oh, boy," I said.

"Oh, what?" He frowned.

"It's Jaz." I winced.

"Okay?" His eyes narrowed.

"Jaz is with your ma," I pointed out.

"Oh, no." He let out a breath. "Better answer it."

"Jaz, what's wrong?" My eyes widened. "We're on our way." I hung up.

"What's up?" He was already standing up.

"Penelope Drakos just came into my parents' restaurant and started a fight with your ma."

No more words were necessary.

CHAPTER 7

"How dare you attack my friend in my place of business," my ma snapped, stabbing a finger in Penelope Drakos' direction as she stood between Penelope and Nik's ma. The restaurant was full of patrons in the middle of the dinner rush, but no one moved or spoke, not even Frona.

Nik and I had just walked through the door, mouths hanging open, as we took in the scene before us.

"Your friend killed my daughter! She walks around town, wearing that family heirloom necklace like she's the Queen of Clearview, and showing off her brand-new house." Penelope shrieked. She was a stunning older version of Ariana, but today her picture-perfect look was a disheveled mess. "While I have a business on the verge of ruin, a dead no-good husband, and my only child murdered. All I have left are her ashes to take home with me. Do you know what that feels like?"

"I can only imagine what you must be going through, but I did no such thing!" Chloe's face was flushed with a mix of outrage and sadness. "Everyone knows I didn't like you or your daughter, but I would never harm anyone."

Jaz slid her arm around Chloe's shoulders and squeezed, glancing over at me with wide helpless eyes.

"I hear talk. You drank the Ouzo from the bottle that hit my daughter in the head and killed her, in your house no less," Penelope drew our attention once more. She held a bottle of wine in her hand as if she planned to do the same to Chloe.

"And I could ask what your daughter was doing in my house in the first place that late at night," Chloe sputtered back.

"There was no forced entry, so you obviously let her in." Penelope waved the bottle, her dark eyes looking crazed.

"I don't remember letting anyone in," Chloe said in a calm voice. "I also didn't take sleeping pills, yet the bottle was laced with them. How do you explain that?"

"Dementia, I say. Drinking and drugs don't mix. You clearly have a problem, and now my beloved child is gone because of it." Penelope's voice broke and she took a step forward. "Someone has to pay."

"Did you ever think someone might be trying to set her up?" my ma added as she side-stepped, keeping herself between Penelope and Chloe with a broom in her hands, ready to react if Penelope made a move.

"Yeah, maybe you!" Penelope jabbed her finger at my ma, and the room gasped as my ma hopped back a step and lifted her broom. "People talk. I hear the rumors. You were jealous Nikos would do the right thing and choose my daughter over yours." Penelope's voice was a hiss now.

My ma snapped her spine straight, her fiery temper beginning to smother her patience. "Your *daughter* claimed she was pregnant with his child when there was never any baby to begin with. Then she came here with her ex-boyfriend. Who does that? At least my child has class."

"The coroner made a mistake." Penelope's eyes went cloudy with doubt. "There *was* a baby. There had to be." She shook off the doubt and raised her voice. "Ariana didn't come here with Benny Balboa. He's a snake, and she knew that. She was genuinely afraid of him and happy to escape the city for a new life with Nikos here in Clearview. She had such high hopes for that. Benny followed her. She can't help that."

"There was *no* baby. I know the truth can be difficult to hear, but it's necessary. Her plan to trap Detective Stevens no work." Ma swiped her hand through the air in a way I'd seen plenty of times, meaning end of discussion. You lose. I win. Conversation over. "I am done with you. Go now."

"I'm not going anywhere, and this is far from over. Your *non*-Greek *adopted* daughter was the only one trying to trap Nikos because she knew she couldn't get anyone else with her weird habits."

"Talk about my daughter one more time, and I show you what this broom can do." Ma's voice dropped to a shiver-inducing tone, her accent more evident with the rise of her blood pressure, as she shoved the broom in Penelope's direction. "I was trying to be nice because no mama wishes the death of a child on anyone, but I grow tired of you and your nonsense. Your daughter, God rest her soul," the entire restaurant made the sign of the cross, "lied to you. And that's that."

"*You* lie. You killed her then tried to cover it up by blaming Nik's ma. Who does *that*?" Penelope's body was tense with rage, her eyes wild with obvious shock still. "And now you're going to pay. All of you." She lunged forward, waving the bottle about.

"That's it." Ma dodged and weaved, waving her broom about. "You want a piece of me? Let's rumble!"

"What is happening?" Chloe squealed as she ran in circles, waving her hands in the air, while Jaz tried to catch her.

"Round and round the bottle goes, who it will hit, nobody knows." Frona skipped about between the tables, singing every step of the way.

Restaurant patrons tried to take cover, while Nik and I made our presence known and did our best to gain control of the room.

"Ma, what are you doing? Come on, put the broom down, please." I made a grab for it and just missed.

"Ms. Stevens, please stop running, you're making me dizzy." Jaz spun in yet another circle and swayed on her feet.

"Mrs. Drakos, give me the bottle. Let me help you. This isn't going to bring Ariana back." Nik worked on cornering Penelope as he talked. "Your actions are going to land you in jail, and none of us want to see that happen after all you've been through."

She wavered a moment, focusing in on him, and then finally she stopped moving all together and burst into tears. "Oh, Nikos, what did my Ariana do to herself?"

Ma and Chloe bounced off of each other, and the broom fell to the floor. Frona picked it up and rode it out of the dining room and into the kitchen with YiaYia chasing after her. The rest of the diners crawled out from beneath their tables and sat in their seats once more while Pop and Papou tried to smooth things over.

Meanwhile, Nik took the bottle from a sobbing

Penelope's hands and set it on a nearby table. He wrapped her in his arms, his expression one of genuine regret. It was obvious he'd cared about Ariana and her ma, no matter what the Dramatic Duo had done to him. The truth hit me hard. Any sort of relationship with one Detective Nik Stevens would have to wait. How long? I had no clue. I just knew I would not be anyone's rebound girl.

Sighing heavily, he answered her question in a soft voice, "I don't know, Penelope, but I can promise you I will find out what happened if it's the last thing I do." His gaze met mine. "For all our sakes."

"Ma, what the heck were you thinking?" I had lingered at my parents' restaurant. Plus, I wasn't ready to face Nik again just yet. I felt like every time we took a step forward, we took two steps back.

A furious Detective Matheson had shown up to take Penelope in for questioning. He'd made it clear that he wasn't happy that drama seemed to follow Detective Stevens, Jaz and me where this case was concerned. Nik took his ma home, and Jaz drove home as well, knowing she was in the doghouse with her boyfriend. I stuck around to try to find out where my ma's head was at.

"What you say?" ma responded, clearly still agitated. "I'm thinking I did a good deed for my friend." Her hands waved about as she talked while scurrying around the empty restaurant and cleaning up the mess they had all made. Boomer had questioned everyone, getting their statements and then making them leave while he sorted it all out. "I'm going to lose so much money from tonight's dinner crowd,"

Ma continued. "All because of that crazy Greek mama."

"Still, Ma...tonight was a disaster."

"Your pop is so upset he called an emergency scrabble game with your papou and Rex back at our house. It's the only thing that helps him relax."

"Rex as in Rex Drummond the mailman?" I arched an eyebrow.

"Yes, that's what I said." She looked at me funny and opened her mouth.

I held up my hand. "No, I don't need aloe for my ears. I'm just surprised because I didn't know they were that friendly with him. He's much younger than them."

"Age-smage. Who cares? The poor man is lonely. They asked him to join their Scrabble Club at the community center once a week. He's not so good, but he seems to like it." She shrugged.

"That's good, I guess." I refocused. "Speaking of being upset. You can't blame Penelope, Ma." I picked up chairs that were turned over and bussed tables while we talked. "You would have gone crazy if anything bad had ever happened to me. You know I'm right."

Her step faltered, and she froze for a moment. "I can't even go there." She shook her head, and her eyes filled with tears. "You are right. No matter what we thought of the Drakos women, they are Greeks, and a child was murdered. We have to figure out what happened so no more of our babies are in harm's way."

"Okay, now you're scaring me." I eyed her warily. "I just wanted you to understand her. One minute you were ready to fight her, and now you're ready to lead the charge."

"Well, someone has to." She got a look in her eye I knew all too well.

I groaned, hoping it wasn't what I thought it was. "What do you have in mind?"

"We must do things our way...the Greek way." Determination laced her voice.

"Oh, no."

"Oh, yes."

I cringed. "You're really going to do this?"

"Yes. I'm left with no choice." She slapped her dishcloth on the bar. "We must band together. It's time to call a meeting of the families."

"GOOD MORNING, NEIGHBOR," I said to Nik the next morning as we stood out back talking over the four-foot-fence that separated our yards.

Nik looked so good in his sport coat, polo, jeans and boots. Yet he looked just as good in shorts and a t-shirt. I had to face it. He looked pretty much amazing at all times. I tucked my blouse into my skirt, drawing his eyes, and I wondered if he was having the same thoughts about me. Taking a sip of my tea, I looked away.

"Good morning to you, friend." He sipped his steaming black brew of coffee, no sugar or artificial sweetener in sight.

I stifled a giggle.

We were having our morning caffeine, trying to salvage our newfound friendship, while our pets were being pets. Wolfgang was digging a hole, trying to squeeze his massive body beneath the fence, while Ms. Priss was perched on my deck railing, ignoring us all as usual. She loved to tease him. One day, that was going to come back to bite her in her furry butt.

"Do you really think someone is trying to set your ma up?" Jaz and Chloe were still sleeping after the traumatic events of yesterday. Speaking of Chloe, I glanced at his half of the house, unable to imagine anyone having anything against such a sweet lady like his ma.

"It's possible. I mean, I've never known her to take sleeping pills, and she's always been able to handle her Ouzo. The question is, what kind of enemies could she have made already?" He scratched his head. "She hasn't even been in town for long."

The early morning dew was drying up as the sun crept higher in the brilliant blue sky, heating things up quickly. It was going to be another hot one.

"If she's anything like my ma, and I'm beginning to see that she is, then it's not completely surprising if she rubbed a couple people the wrong way. Did you ask her if she made any enemies?"

"I did, actually." He rubbed his jaw, looking uncomfortable. "Let's just say, since Ma and Pop split, she has been on the hunt for a man."

"Really?" I felt my skin grow warm. "I mean, it makes sense. Your ma is a beautiful woman."

He held up his hand. "Don't even go there. I can't have the image in my brain of my ma flirting with men."

"Well, you're the one who brought it up." I chuckled and eyed him curiously. "Why is that, anyway?"

"Because there might be some truth to what you said."

I feigned surprised and slapped my hand on my chest. "Do tell."

He rolled his eyes. "It has unfortunately come to my attention that ma is a member of a singles club here in Clearview."

Genuine surprise hit me this time. "Oh, that's wonderful. Good for her." I clapped my hands.

He cringed. "Not good for her or wonderful for me. At any rate, there is a widow woman who likes Captain Crenshaw."

"Oh, you mean, Nina Simone." I waved my hand in the air, dismissing his worry. "That woman has been trying to turn Captain Crenshaw's eye for a long time now. There's nothing to worry about there."

"You're mistaken. There's definitely something to worry about there. The woman has had zero success with the captain for years. Now that my ma is in town, it only took her a couple days to lock him in for a dinner date."

I choked on my coffee. "Seriously?"

"I'm dead serious. Let's just say it didn't go over well with Nina. All of this went down before my ma even moved to town. Here I thought she was following me by moving to Clearview. Now, I think it had more to do with the captain than anything else."

"Wow, that's crazy. I mean, I'm happy for your ma, but everyone loves Nina. Her husband served with Crenshaw in the military when they were young. Then years later, Simone joined the force only to die in the line of duty. That's probably why Crenshaw never said yes to Nina, out of respect for her late husband."

"It doesn't really matter what the reason is. All I know is he said yes to my ma right away, and that didn't sit well with the widow."

"How do you know?"

"I guess Nina confronted my ma and made it clear

that if Ma went through with the date, the widow would make her regret it."

My jaw fell open. "Does your ma have proof?"

"Of course not. The widow made sure all her threats were never in writing."

"Great. That brings us back to square one."

"Not exactly. At least now we have a suspect to question. And several of Ma's neighbors have front door cameras we can check."

"That's true. At least that's something."

Just then, I heard a rustling behind me. I turned around and Wolfgang's head emerged, followed quickly by his body from beneath my half of the fence.

I gasped.

Nik yelled.

Wolfgang ran.

Ms. Priss let out a meow that could make the chill bumps on the top of your head tingle.

And then chaos ensued.

Wolfy chased Prissy around the yard, barking and howling and whining with a mix of adoration and excitement. Prissy scrambled up the highest tree she could. Jaz and Chloe came running outside, looking thoroughly confused. Nik scolded to no avail. And then the unthinkable happened.

Wolfgang trained his eyes on me.

"Don't you even think about it, Mister!" I yelled.

For once, the massive St. Bernard didn't listen.

I started to run, and he followed.

I screamed, he squealed.

I scrambled up my deck and thought I had reached safety.

Wolfgang caught up to me before I could open the door.

Standing on his back paws, he framed my face

with his front paws and stuck out his tongue. His long, wet, dripping with saliva and germs monstrosity that he proceeded to bathe my face with.

I screamed at the top of my lungs.

His eyes went wide, his expression filled with horror, and he ran for his life.

Smart dog.

"You'd better run, you bad boy!" I gagged. "After I thoroughly shower and apply antiseptic, you are in so much trouble."

He scrambled under the hole beneath the fence faster than I thought possible.

"And you!" I thrust my finger at a gaping, horrified Nik.

He held up his hands and shook his head in apology.

"Oh, no. You're not getting off that easy. You and your naughty boy are both in the doghouse! And don't think you're coming out any time soon."

CHAPTER 8

"I am head of the family, Ophelia," my pop, Amos, said in our Greek restaurant after hours. "I will run this meeting." The music was turned off, and he stood behind the bar as if it were a judge's desk, with a gavel before him. Everyone else sat at the tables surrounding the bar area.

"You might be the head, but you know I turn the head any which way I want." Ma crossed her arms and dared him to say otherwise. She pursed her lips, not looking pleased with him at the moment.

We all knew Ma was in charge. It was true, but we were in front of the Ballas as well as the Pagonis families, and she was embarrassing him. My pop stood straighter, barely taller than my ma, his thick hair now thinning with a bald spot in the back and his stomach now rounded from years of sampling the menu. My adopted Greek self stood taller than them both, and I wasn't even that tall.

Pop whacked a gavel down hard on the bar, snapping everyone's attention back toward him. He puffed out his chest, trying with all his might to look authoritative. "The direction you've headed in has caused nothing but trouble for this family and this business." He held up the broom she'd recently swung about like a sword. "Now sit down, woman, and let me speak for once."

The room grew Sunday mass quiet.

Ma gasped.

"Please," Pop added, mouthing, *Sorry*.

Aunt Tasoula made the sign of the cross.

After a tense moment, Ma sat, and you could hear a room full of sighs of relief. I think she knew he needed that moment to shine, so she let him have it. But you could be sure she would give him an earful later.

"As head of the Ballas family, I called this gathering because one of our own needs our help. We don't turn our backs on our fellow Greeks." He stepped to the side and Penelope Drakos walked forward.

The room looked shocked, a rare moment of silence, then everyone started talking at once.

"What is she doing here? She accused me of murder," Chloe said, standing up in a ready position.

"Yeah, and her daughter stole my clients and tried to ruin me," Thalia added, joining her in a united front.

"I know, ladies. She caused damage to this very restaurant, and I, too, have been wrongly accused," my ma cut in. "No matter what happened in the past, we have to understand why. Someone murdered her child. I can't imagine what I would do if that happened to me." Ma gave me a quick hug before letting go.

A tense moment filled the room, and then Chloe and Thalia sat back down.

Chloe looked at Nik while nodding her head.

"She's right. I would go a little crazy for sure." Her gaze settled on Penelope. She still didn't look thrilled, but she shrugged. "It's time for a truce. Greeks help Greeks."

"Thank you all. I don't know what to say. I lost my mind for a while. I can admit that. This whole thing has just been really difficult for me." Penelope dabbed a handkerchief at the corners of her eyes. "After so much bad blood between us, I never imagined we would all work together."

"It's what we do," Pop said, whacking the gavel for good measure.

Ma rolled her eyes, then stood and clapped her hands. "Okay, the show's over. First, we eat. Then we talk strategy."

Eleni, Ma, YiaYia Dido, and I all brought trays of food out to line the bar while my cousins Kosmos and Silas served everyone. Nik's uncles and aunts and cousins went first, followed by Pop, Papou Homer, Nik and Penelope.

Frona skipped about with her plastic tub to bus tables as people finished, sometimes tossing full plates of unfinished food in the bin. YiaYia would scurry behind her, apologizing and fetching a new plate of food.

Frona's mom died years ago and my uncle couldn't handle her on his own, so YiaYia stepped up to take care of her, getting her a job at my parents' restaurant washing dishes in the back. Getting her to stay in the back was the biggest issue, but pretty much everyone in town knew Frona and made allowances because she was always fun, happy, and harmless.

I filled a plate and headed out into the restaurant. Nik motioned for me to join him and Penelope, but I pretended not to see. I sat with Ma and Chloe, not ready to forgive Nik just yet. Memories of Wolfgang bathing my face were still too fresh. My stomach turned over, so I pushed the food around on my plate, pretending to eat as I listened. Ma and Chloe were talking about the singles club and how Captain Crenshaw hadn't called Chloe since the murder. That got me thinking about the widow, Nina Simone.

Maybe it was time I stepped out of my comfort zone and joined a club. My gaze settled on Nik, and as if he were drawn to me, his baby blues locked with mine. Ignoring the butterflies in my stomach, I knew what I had to do. Because like it or not...

I was most definitely single.

I COULDN'T BELIEVE IT. The Singles' Club was held in the back party room of Rosalita's Place. I knew Rosalita and her Mexican restaurant was one of the few places I would eat. Rosalita's Place had a southwestern theme and the best margaritas. Her authentic Mexican cuisine was second to none.

This was the same restaurant where I had gone with Jaz a couple months ago, as her wingwoman, while she met her internet date, Darin, who later was murdered and she had been the prime suspect. Jaz had fixed me up on a blind date, and I'd discovered pretty quickly he was the nice Greek boy my ma had been trying to fix me up with for weeks.

Aka Detective Nikos Stevens.

Squashing down the memories, I pulled out a sanitized wipe and opened the door, then tossed the wipe into a trash can. I tried to inconspicuously make my way to the back room without being seen, gearing myself up for how many hands I might have to shake. I wondered if my single prospects would be offended if

I asked them to wash their hands first. It was a known fact that many people didn't wash their hands after going to the bathroom, and those who did wash, didn't wash long enough to actually kill germs.

This was such a bad idea. I was going to look like a freak.

"Hey, Kalli, what are you doing here?" Rosalita asked, spotting me. I stifled a groan. We'd gone to high school together. She was a feisty, fun woman with curves in all the right places and the best hair in the entire county.

I waved, smoothing down the summer sundress Jaz had made me wear. I always felt so strange with my hair down, but Jaz had insisted I look the part if I was going to spy on the Singles' Club. "Hi, Rosi. I'm here for the Singles' Club meeting."

Her hazel eyes sprang wide. "You?"

I stood a little straighter and tried not to squirm in my dress. "Yes, me. Why do you sound so shocked? Do I look bad?"

"Not at all, I'm just surprised to see you at this club."

"I date."

"Exactly. I guess I thought you were already dating Detective Stevens." She leaned forward as if divulging a scandal. "I mean, half the town did see you two kiss. You know how news spreads around here."

"Yes, well, half the town also saw his ex-girlfriend storm in and claim he was the father of her baby not long after that kiss."

"But you two look so cute together, and I heard that baby news wasn't true," she said. "So, you're free to date him again, right?" She smiled wide as if it were all that simple. Maybe for most people it would be that simple. But I wasn't most people.

"It's complicated, Rosi." I nodded my head once. "We both agreed to focus on helping his ma and just be friends. No time for dating right now."

She squinted. "Then what are you doing here?"

I couldn't tell her I was doing a little unofficial investigating of my own, especially after promising Nik we would work together, but there was no way I was going to have him go with me to a singles' club. That would defeat the purpose. So, I channeled my inner Jaz. "Oh, well, Nik's with his ma, and I needed a break." I feigned an excited smile. "I heard this club was a lot of fun and not too serious, so I thought why not."

She raised a brow. "Um, okay, whatever you're into." She pointed to the back. "Better hurry up. They're almost done."

I took a deep breath, then hurried through the restaurant hoping I didn't see anyone I knew as I headed to the door in the back. Pasting a smile on my face, I waited until someone walked out and then I stepped inside the room. And stopped. And stared.

No one told me this was a singles' club for seniors!

I was about to turn around and escape when Captain Crenshaw spotted me. He set his jaw and headed in my direction.

Oh, boy. I popped a hip and acted like it was perfectly normal for me to be there. "Hi, Captain. Fancy meeting you here." I threw in a hair toss for good measure.

He cocked an eyebrow. "Is it though? Funny that I can't say the same for you." He placed his hands on his hips. "Ms. Ballas, what are you doing here?"

Looking for the widow Simone, I wanted to say, but that would give the real reason I was here away. That I was snooping in places I didn't belong. "Why, what a silly question, Captain. I imagine I'm here for the same reason everyone else is." I lied.

A few ears perked up at that and started making their way in my direction. Oh lord, what had I gotten myself into? It wasn't just people in their seventies and eighties. I swallowed hard. There were people in their forties, fifties, and sixties as well. Like Captain Crenshaw for one. He was a good-looking man with his salt and pepper buzzcut and steel gray eyes. But still. I wasn't quite thirty and not looking for a new daddy figure.

"Right," he said, clearly not buying my story.

"Hey, is Nina Simone here?" I searched the room. "I heard she might be sweet on you." I elbowed him and winked.

He frowned.

I cleared my voice. "She's a good-looking woman for sure."

"Who happened to be married to my best friend. I don't want to date her, but I don't want to upset her, either."

"Why? Was she upset when you asked Chloe out instead? Do you happen to know where she was on the night of Ariana's murder?" I bit my bottom lip. Maybe I'd gone a little too far on my questioning. I was new to investigating, after all, and had to admit it was harder than I had thought.

He rubbed his jaw and studied me. "If you lied to me and you're here butting your nose into the murder case, I'm going to have to haul you in."

"Nope, I was just curious, that's all, because Chloe said you haven't called her since the murder." I held up my hands. "I'm not here to judge. I'm just looking out for my friend, that's all. I promise." I peeked beyond him. "Oh, look. I see a few prospects waiting to talk to me, so I'll let you go mingle, Captain. Good luck."

I quickly walked past him and stumbled when I spotted Rex Drummond. He did a double-take, his face flamed bright red, then he did an about face and fairly flew out the door. The poor guy really was a basket case around women. Or maybe just around me. I wasn't certain, but I was sure my pop and papou had most likely sent him here in hopes of helping him out. They probably never imagined I would be here. I sighed. I was never going to live this down.

I glanced over my shoulder and saw the captain still staring at me, so I kept moving and headed over to a group of men I recognized quite well: Larry Miller, Gary Bolin, and Ronald Banks.

Larry ran the Clearview Motel. He was in his sixties, with a thinning combover, bulbous nose, too-small eyes, and small round spectacles. He loved to complain about his gout and reminisce about the old days. When he barked out a laugh, you could see he was missing a couple molars.

Ronald Banks was in his fifties but looked much older from his years of working in the sun, his skin a dark tan with a leathered texture. He ran Banks Construction. He was a short stocky man with a bald head and glasses. I wasn't that tall, but I could easily see over the top of his shiny head.

Gary Bolin was the closest to my age at forty, but he was a regular at Flannigan's pub and drunk way too often. He was out of work and still living with his mother, his dirty blond hair in desperate need of a cut, but he had nice green eyes. Too bad they were always bloodshot. Still, if I was desperate, he was a far cry better than Missing Molars Miller or Baldy Banks.

"Gotta say, I didn't expect to see you here," Gary

said with only a slight slur to his words, swaying toward me. "I thought you and Stevens were a thing."

I leaned back. "Nope, definitely not anything but friends."

"You don't say." Larry grinned, and I tried not to cringe over the gaps in his teeth. "I get it. I have plenty of friends, but I get lonely too sometimes." He stared at my eyes. "You lonely, Ms. Ballas?"

"Oh, no, I'm fine."

"Then what are you doing here?" Ronald sized me up, looking suspicious. "You shouldn't be leading people on and wasting their time. That's not right."

"Oh, no, I'm not leading anyone on, I promise. I am just looking to have some fun. You know who *is* lonely though. The widow, Nina Simone."

"Don't bother with her." Larry grunted. "I tried to talk to her once, but she only has eyes for the captain."

"That maybe have been true at one time, but not since he made it clear he wouldn't date her," Ronald replied. "I think he's got eyes on someone else."

"That's true," Gary chimed in. "I saw Ms. Simone with that new guy. The one that used to date the girl that got whacked." Gary snapped his fingers. "Balboa. They were at Flannigan's Pub a couple days ago."

"But she's way older than him," I said.

They looked at each other and then at me.

"Age is just a number to some people," Gary said. "She has plenty of money. For some people, that's reason enough." He moved slowly toward me with a goofy grin spreading across his face. "I heard your naughty nighty business is doing well. If you need for me to model any of them for me, I'm your man."

"I'll keep that in mind." I stepped back further from him, feeling the need to shower. Being gainfully employed would go a long way in helping Gary find a woman, but picturing him anywhere near my *naughty nighties,* as he'd put it, made my skin crawl. "Well, gentleman, it's been lovely getting to know you all, but I have to run." I turned around and headed to the door. "Don't call me, I'll call you."

"But you don't have our number," Gary hollered back. He started to follow me across the floor.

"No worries. I definitely have *your* number." I tried not to shudder as I picked up the pace on my way out the door.

Glancing behind me, I didn't stop moving until I was sure I'd lost him. I knew I could beat him in a footrace if I had to, even in these toothpicks for heels. But for a minute, I could have sworn someone was watching me. I glanced around again and held my keys in my hand like a weapon, but I didn't see anything so I unlocked my Prius and tried to put my suitors behind me. Thank goodness another thought occupied my mind....

What was Benny Balboa up to now?

CHAPTER 9

I waited until Friday night when I knew Flannigan's Pub would be hopping. I'd donned a summer sundress, sandals, and left my hair down. I glanced at my watch. Jaz was late. We were supposed to have a girl's night. Jaz told me I needed one, and I was hoping to run into Nina Simone since she'd last been spotted here. No one had seen her since the night she was seen with Benny at this very bar. I wiped off a stool and sat down.

"Hey, cuz." Silas joined me at the bar moments later, flashing his famous dimples at the bartender and signaling for her to poor him another round. He added a glass of wine for me without even having to ask my order.

My family knew me so well.

Michael Flannigan was no fool. He'd known he would make way more money off hiring Zena Renner as a bartender. She was all of five-foot-two, with a willowy figure, a short blonde pixie haircut, and lavender eyes. For as tiny as she was, her personality was twice her size and her smile even bigger. She was about the only woman who could hold her own against a flirt like Silas. She set a glass of wine before me then moved back down the bar.

"Hey yourself." I smiled at my cousin, checking my glass for fingerprints or lipstick stains. Only when I was positive it was clean, did I take a sip.

"Gotta say, I'm surprised to see you here. And alone? That's not the Kalli I know." He tweaked my nose.

I swatted his hand away. "Funny. I'm not here alone. I'm waiting for Jaz." I sighed. "I love that girl, but she's always late."

"True." He laughed. "But that's a woman who's worth the wait."

A beer slid down the bar, coming to a stop directly in front of Silas without a single drop spilling. We both looked down the bar in surprise. Zena winked at Silas, flashed her own dimples, all the while mixing more drinks without missing a beat.

Silas stared as if transfixed.

"Speaking of women who are worth the wait, I think you've finally found your match." I nudged him with my shoulder as I chuckled.

"That's crazy talk right there." He tore his guilty gaze away from her and took a long sip from his beer.

"You're blushing."

"Yup, you've definitely gone mad. There isn't a woman out there who can handle all this." He swept his hand down his long, lean frame.

"Or one who would want to." Kosmos joined us at the bar on my other side. He already had a whiskey neat in his muscular hand. His sleepy bedroom eyes danced with amusement as he took a sip.

"You're just jealous." Silas grinned.

"Yeah, that's my problem. I've always wanted to be like you, little brother." Kosmos rolled his eyes, then focused on me. "I'm glad to see you, cuz, but I'm kind of surprised you're here. I thought you were with Detective Stevens?"

"Nope, not with him. Definitely single." I took a bigger drink of my wine, then patted my lips dry three times with the sanitized cocktail napkin I'd brought with me.

"Speaking of single," Silas jumped back in, "why in Hades would you go to the Singles Club for a date? Our generation dates online. Don't get me wrong, Rosalita's is a great restaurant. But meeting in an actual room should have been your first clue what kind of singles you would meet. Chat rooms are more our generation's speed."

"I don't want to date anyone. Been there, done that, didn't work out so well with my quirks." Amen to that.

"The way I see it, anyone who can't see what an amazing woman you are isn't worth your time." Kosmos took another sip of his whiskey, his tone as warm and sincere as the amber liquid, then his lips tipped up just a little.

"Thanks, Kos. That means a lot." My heart warmed. No matter how crazy my family might be, they always had each other's backs.

"What's up, Yanni. Haven't seen you out in forever," Silas said as yet another one of my cousin's joined us. "How's business?"

Yanni was a little older, in his forties, but still as handsome as the rest of my cousins. He was a little more weathered because of all the long hours working in the sun for his landscaping business, Yanni's Yards. His business had grown as Clearview had grown, and he was finally able to expand.

"Business is booming. This is the new guy I told you all about, Erik Thompson. I hired him a month ago. Best decision I ever made. These are my crazy cousins Silas, Kosmos, and the lovely Kalliope." He winked at me. "Erik has done some great work for me already. You've probably seen his work around town."

Erik was probably around the same age as Yanni, with a full dark brown beard and short ponytail. Too much facial hair freaked me out a little bit because food could get caught in the scruff. I forced my eyes up and smiled. He shrugged, flushing over the praise. "Just doing my job." He nodded to us. "Nice to meet you all."

"I saw the job you did at Chloe Steven's new house. The landscaping with the gazebo out back looks amazing," I said. "There's a lot of pressure in designing a back yard for a Greek family and their Sunday brunches."

"Yeah, I've come to see that since moving to Clearview." He let out a little laugh. "There's, um, a lot of you in town."

"Twice as many since the Pagonis family moved here. It's hard not to feel outnumbered, I imagine."

"It's okay. Everyone I've met has been really friendly."

Speaking of people who were new in town, Benny Balboa walked in and headed straight to the bar.

"If you'll excuse me gentlemen, I need to use the ladies' room." I walked toward the restroom until my nosy, protective family stopped watching me, then I pivoted toward the bar. Coming to a stop behind Benny, I watched him flirt with Zena.

"Benny Balboa, you certainly are making the rounds during your stay in Clearview, aren't you," I said quietly near his ear.

He twisted his barstool around until he sat sideways. "Back for more, I see. Couldn't get enough of me the first time?"

"Oh, I'm pretty sure I had my fill of you. One encounter is enough for a lifetime. More than one didn't work out so well for Ariana Drakos."

His eyes hardened, and I felt his icy stare clear to my bones. I'd thought confronting him in a room full of people would be safe, but now I wasn't so sure. I swallowed hard and tried to hide my fear. "What I do with my personal life is none of your business. Tread lightly, Ballas. Your big detective isn't here to protect you."

"I don't need him. Look around, Balboa. I'm related to half the people in this bar. All I have to do is say the word, and they'll be all over you like flies on the pile of garbage that you are."

"You don't want to bring the *family* into this. Yours wouldn't stand a chance against mine."

"Is that what happened to the widow Simone? No one has seen Nina around since she was with you here. Did you have your *family* take care of her?"

"Don't speak about things you know nothing of. I don't like being wrongfully accused, little girl." He stood until he was taller than me, then leaned forward until I could feel his breath on my face. "Your family can't be with you twenty-four seven. Better watch your back, Ballas. I'm watching you."

"Kalli, there you are," came a voice I recognized from behind me. "Sorry I'm late. I got here as soon as I could."

I blinked.

The voice did *not* belong to Jaz. I turned around and my eyes sprang wide. Something had to be wrong with my vision. I'd have to see Doc LaLone soon. Gary Bolin stood before me, looking like a completely different man and at least ten years younger. He'd cut his hair, the dirty blond strands looking more like sun and sand as they fell in waves around the top of his head, the sides fading into a tightly edged line around his ears and neck. His green eyes looked like a sharper emerald without being bloodshot. He wore slim cut jeans with a light green t-shirt tucked in and trendy sneakers.

Gary Bolin was hot.

I couldn't find my voice as I stared with my mouth agape.

"Excuse us, Benny, but this one's already taken for the evening." Gary held out his arm, and I linked mine through it in a numb state of shock. "Come on, Kalli, I'll walk you to your car."

We walked out the doors of Flannigan's Pub and headed toward my car.

"I...I...don't know what to say." I cleared the croaking from my voice.

"You looked like you needed an out. Balboa isn't someone you mess with." Gary shoved his hands in his jean pockets.

"Thank you. He's definitely scary." I looked Gary over, still shocked. "I'm sorry for staring. You look so different. In a good way."

"I figured it was time I got a job. There's a reason I am the way I am, but I don't talk about that. I'm just thankful for my mother these past few years, but it's time I got back on my feet. Larry hired me as the new face of the Clearview Motel. I figured I'd better clean up my act and look the part so I don't let him down." *And now that I'm gainfully employed, I'm hoping I stand a chance with her. She was so nice when she talked to me. Most women don't give me the time of day. Oh, man, I hope she gives me a shot. I won't let her down, either.*

I let go of his arm as we reached my Prius. "Good for you, Gary. I'm sure you'll do a great job. Thank you for making sure I reached my car safe and sound." I scanned the parking lot to make sure Benny hadn't followed us.

"You're welcome." He shoved his hands in his pockets again as I got in my car and rolled down the window. "Hey, are you free for coffee tomorrow? No pressure, just coffee. We can meet at Sinfully Delicious in the morning if that works?" His green eyes looked so hopeful and sincere. How could I say no? I owed him after tonight.

"Sure. I'll meet you there at eight. Thanks again." I left my window open and headed home in a daze. Being gainfully employed wasn't the only thing helping Gary find a woman. Transforming from the town drunk ragdoll into this month's clean-cut centerfold just increased his odds exponentially.

The question was, what was I prepared to do about it?

~

"You sure you want to do this?" Jaz asked the next morning as we were both getting ready to leave for work.

"If you didn't stand me up last night, I wouldn't have needed Gary to walk me to my car," I pointed out as I fed Prissy her premium cat food in her fancy dish. Then and only then would she eat.

"I didn't stand you up. I told you, Tammy never showed up for the closing shift, and Debbie wasn't available. I can't seem to find good help. I swear, no one wants to work these days." Jaz put her coffee cup in the sink. "In my defense, I sent you a text to which you never responded. And you left without making sure I wasn't on my way."

"Yeah, my phone died. I really do need to get better at making sure it's charged before I go places. I'm just not used to going out."

"Which leads me back to my original question. Are you sure you want to do this? There still might be a chance for you and Detective Dreamy if you would allow it. But once you start dating someone else, it's harder to come back from that. Believe me I know. I just don't want you to have the same regrets I did."

Jaz had fallen hard for Boomer, and it had terrified her. So, she'd pushed him away and dated pretty much everyone else in town. That caused a rift between them for over a year. After she'd nearly gone to prison for a murder she didn't commit, she reevaluated what was important to her. Boomer finally wore her down, and they'd been together ever since. She'd gotten lucky. I didn't think the result would be the same for me. It never was.

I twisted my hair into its usual knot and straightened my suit, feeling more confident like this. "There is no Nik and me. Besides, this isn't a date. I'm simply having coffee with a friend as a thank you for helping me. That's all."

"Did you tell him that?"

"Quit worrying."

"What if he tries to kiss you?"

I thought about that. "You know what, I wouldn't mind." Her eyes widened in surprise. "I know it sounds crazy, but part of me wants to know if *any* man can make me forget my own thoughts because of my gift, or if it's exclusive to Detective Dreamy. Since we're not dating, this might be my chance to find out."

"If you say so, but I still think you're going to regret this."

Ten minutes later, I headed out my front door. I hadn't really talked to Nik since the whole Wolfgang assault. Not because I was mad for real. I just hadn't had the time. He stood out front with Wolfgang on a leash, getting ready to put him in his truck.

"Hey, Kalli," his honey smooth voice was rich and oozy as it tickled my insides, same as always.

"Hi, Nik. It's good to see you." I smiled and meant it.

"How are you? Really? Better, I hope." He winced, glancing down at his beast. "Wolf is sorry, by the way."

As if on cue, Wolfgang hung his massive head, peaking up at me and looking pitiful.

I sighed. "I forgive you."

He popped up, his body quivering with excitement, and his huge tongue rolled out.

I held up a hand in a stay position. "Put that nasty thing back in your mouth when you're around me."

As if he understood every word, his tongue disappeared and his fanny plopped down hard on the blacktop.

"Good boy." I walked over, and he didn't move an inch. Just a soft whine emerged from deep in his throat. I lifted my hand and pet the top of his head, even circling his ears. His whine turned to a moan, but he behaved himself like a gentleman should. "Maybe next time, I'll scratch your back." He flopped down and rolled over. "Sorry, buddy, you could be a saint, but I draw the line at belly rubs." I shuddered just thinking of the dirt and Lord knew what else he rolled in on a daily basis.

"I hope that means I'm forgiven too," Nik said. "I promise he won't escape into your yard ever again."

"Of course, you're forgiven. We need to compare notes on anything new we found out since we last talked."

"How about now?" Nik asked. "I have to drop Wolf off at Dino's Doggy Daycare, but then I'm free."

"I'm not." I chewed my bottom lip, the neckline of my shirt suddenly feeling too tight. This was silly. We were just friends.

"Oh? Got a hot date," Nik teased.

"I wouldn't call it a date," I replied, not quite meeting his eyes.

He stopped moving. "Oh." His tone turned somber. "I see."

"It's just coffee to say thank you to Gary Bolin for coming to my rescue last night." *Whoops.*

Nik had most definitely turned back into Detective Stevens. "Excuse me? Wanna repeat that?"

Not really. "It was nothing. I went out to Flannigan's Pub to have drinks with Jaz for a girls' night, but she never showed. My cousins were there, teasing me about going to the Single's Club—"

"Wait, what?" Detective Stevens' frown deepened.

I swiped my hand through the air. "I didn't realize it was a senior singles group, but that's another story."

"I thought you weren't dating at all."

"I wasn't. I mean, I'm not. It has to do with the case, but never mind that. I'm talking about last night at the bar."

"That's not much better, Ballas." I knew he was getting mad when he called me by my last name.

I took a deep breath, held it as I counted to ten, and then blew it out. "Listen, I'm on my way to have coffee with Gary to thank him for walking me to my car last night after Benny threatened me."

"What?" The detective's jaw bulged, making him

not look so dreamy at the moment and he fisted his hands.

"It's not a big deal. That's all that happened."

"That's plenty." Detective Stevens put Wolf in his truck and got in without saying another word.

Now I was the one to ask, "Where are you going?"

He rolled down his window, the anger rolling off him in waves. "It's not a big deal. Nothing's gonna happen," he threw my words back at me. "I'll fill you in like you did me, *after* the fact." He put his truck in reverse and peeled out of the driveway.

Jaz's words came back to me. *I think you're going to regret this.*

Why did she always have to be right?

CHAPTER 10

Sinfully Delicious was Maria Danza's bakery, right across the street from Full Disclosure, which was very convenient for Jaz and I since Maria's pastries were the best. At one point, Maria didn't like Jaz because Jaz had dated Johnny Hogan, and that was Maria's ex-boyfriend. But after Johnny turned out to be a loser, the women called a truce. And now that Maria was dating the delivery guy, Sully Anderson, and Jaz was dating Detective Boomer Matheson, the two women had actually become friends.

I arrived before Gary, so I waited by the counter. "Hey, Maria, how's the family?" Maria was from a big Italian family, so she had always been able to relate to what it was like to have 24/7 drama, and a ma who constantly forced food at you while trying to fix you up with the appropriate guy.

"Oh, same as always. You know how it is." She rolled her dark expressive eyes and flipped her long black ponytail over her shoulder. Her cherubic cheeks had a rosy glow. "How's yours?"

I laughed. "Worse than always. It's double the amount of drama with the Pagonis family in town."

"Yeah, Jaz told me about what has been going on. Poor Chloe Stevens. And now you all are helping Penelope Drakos?" One of her eyebrows crept up high. "How did that come about? I thought they all hated each other?"

"She's Greek." I shrugged. "That means she's one of our own, and apparently, that's enough."

Sully came in carrying a package and handed it to Maria. He kissed her cheek, and she blushed, her face beaming with happiness. He was tall, with curly caramel hair and a winning smile. I was happy for them both.

"That's for Lisa," he said, then smiled at me. "Gotta run, ladies. Duty calls." He turned and left as quickly as he'd arrived in his khaki shirt and shorts, then drove away in his dark brown delivery van.

Lisa Chamberlain had been hired as a bookkeeper for Maria for the past few months. She'd really helped her turn her business around since she'd arrived. Maria said she didn't know how her shop had survived without Lisa. She was a godsend at organization and a whiz at numbers.

Lisa came out from a door in the back room, looked around for a moment, then asked, "Did I just hear Sully?"

"Yes, he left this for you." Maria handed her a package.

"Oh, good. I was expecting a delivery and was hoping it would come today." Lisa took the package.

"What is it?" Maria asked.

"Oh, just some things I used at my former job that I think will really help take this place to a new level." She turned to head back into the back room but then she spotted me. "Oh, hi, Kalli. Here for your usual?" She grinned.

"You girls know me well." I didn't eat at many places unless I was positive the kitchen was clean. Maria always put extra care into the items she made and packaged for me, and I so appreciated that. "I'm waiting for someone first."

Lisa's brow puckered. "I thought I passed Detective Stevens headed in the opposite direction when I got here a little while ago."

"I'm not meeting the detective."

There was a pause as the women looked at each other.

"You're not?" Maria finally asked.

Gary Bolin walked in at that moment. He looked around, smiled when he saw me, and headed in our direction.

"Oh," Lisa said. "Oh, my, who's that." She fanned her face when Gary came to a stop by me.

"Ladies." He nodded.

"Gary?" Maria gaped.

He chuckled. "Yes, it's really me. Don't worry, you're not the first one to give me that reaction."

"I'm sorry, you just look so different."

"So, I've heard." He smiled.

"He got a job," I said, proud of him.

"Well, good for you. Work is so important, don't you think? I mean, I think that's just grand. You must be thrilled." Lisa stammered on, looking flustered and more than a little besotted. She was a pretty brunette and around his age by the look of it. "Wh-Where are you working?" She cleared her throat.

Gary eyed her a little funny, not used to women giving him the time of day, I was sure. "I'm the new face of the Clearview Motel. Larry is still in charge. He just wants to be more behind the scenes now since he's getting on up there in years."

"We're here to celebrate," I said.

His face flushed as if he just remembered me, and he fidgeted in his new clothes. "I'll just get us a table."

"I'll be right there," I said and turned to the ladies when he left. "Before you ask, no it's not a date."

"Oh?" Lisa's face looked relieved, then she shifted her stance. "I mean, whatever it is, I hope you have a nice day." The bell over the front door chimed, and Lisa looked in that direction. Penelope Drakos walked in and headed to the far end of the counter by Maria, and Lisa ducked.

"Are you okay?" I peeked around the corner behind the counter, a little startled over the change in Lisa's behavior.

"I'm fine. Dropped my earring. Gotta get back to work." She picked up her box, kept low, and hustled to the back room.

I stood back up and waved to an oblivious Penelope. She waved back, completed her order, and then left. How bizarre, I thought, and couldn't wait to tell Nik, but then I spotted Gary at our table, still waiting for me, and my heart sank.

You're going to regret this....

"Shut up," I said as I reached the table.

"But I didn't say anything." Gary looked at me with wary green eyes.

"Sorry, not you."

He looked around me. "Then who?"

I waved a hand. "Oh, just the voices in my head."

"Fair enough," he said. "No judgement here. I've had a few of those myself. Never did like what they had to say, but I guess I finally listened."

Once more the bell chimed as the front door opened. Nik walked inside, ordered a large black coffee extra strong and met my gaze once before walking back out. But I'd only needed one look to see the start of a black eye.

I let out a heavy sigh as I replied, "I'm beginning to think maybe I should start."

~

WHAT A LONG DAY. I was getting nowhere with clearing Chloe's name, and I was getting nowhere with creating new designs. So, I left work early. Nik pulled in just as I did. We both parked and got out of our cars.

"What did you do?" I asked him as I looked at his ever-darkening eye, crossing my arms over my chest and waiting for an explanation.

He winced. "I ran into a wall."

I picked up his hand and examined the red, swollen knuckles. "And then punched it for hitting you in the eye?"

"Something like that." *This friend thing is killing me. I can't stand the thought of anyone dating you, let alone threatening you.*

"We're not dating." I dropped his hand.

"So, you've said."

"I mean, I'm not dating anyone else. As in Gary and I are not dating."

"Oh." He lifted a shoulder as if trying to act like it didn't matter.

"Can we pick up where we left off?" I asked.

His face brightened. "You mean go on our first date?"

"No, I mean compare notes like we planned to."

"Yeah, sure." His smile dimmed. "I'll meet you at my place in five minutes if that works for you?"

"Sounds good."

I headed into my half of the house, dropped my

stuff, and immediately sanitized my hands three times. Prissy lounged lazily on the back of the couch. I fed her and after she ate, she whined to go out back, so I let her out. She loved to sun herself on the deck railing and tease Wolfgang.

After changing out of my work clothes into running shorts and a tank top, I peeked out at Prissy to tell her to stop teasing Wolfy. His whine was pathetic, but he wasn't whining at her. He was staring at the back fence.

Shrugging, I left the door open for my cat in case she wanted back inside, then I headed over to Nik's house. I barely knocked, and he let me inside. He wore athletic shorts and a tank top as well. The temperature had been scorching today.

"Come on in. Ma's in the sunroom."

I walked through his house and saw Chloe looking as fresh as ever. "You look well rested."

"I just woke up from a nap. I love my naps. Because I don't sleep well at night, I sleep like the dead during my naps."

"I wish I could nap. I've never been able to." I sat down and looked out the back window. Wolfgang still sat in the same place.

"Would you like a glass of wine?" Nik asked.

I loved that he kept my favorite on hand. Although, I kept his favorite beer at Jaz and my house as well. "Sure, that would be lovely."

"We'll go out on the deck and talk, that way we won't disturb Ma."

"You're not disturbing me, but I planned a nice dinner for you both. It's not quite ready. Let me work on that while you kids talk. I didn't expect you back this early."

Nik and I went out back and sat down.

"You should have seen Lisa Chamberlain at the bakery today. She got all flushed when Gary came in with his new look. I think she likes him."

Nik grunted and took a swig of his beer. I didn't have to read his mind to know he didn't want to talk about other guys who liked me.

"Anyway, Penelope Drakos came in, and Lisa acted so strangely. She ducked, and when I asked her about it, she said she dropped an earring. Then she made an excuse and headed to the back room. Penelope didn't see her. What do you think it means?"

"Ariana stirred up trouble all over town before her death. Even with Maria in demanding a ridiculous cake for the wedding." He looked me in the eye. "A wedding that was never going to be, mind you. That was probably it."

"Oh, maybe. So did you find out anything more?" I sipped my wine.

"The neighbors door cams showed Nina Simone at ma's house, looking like they were arguing, but that's it. She never went inside."

"And I asked some of her friends about her, but no one seems to have seen her since she was with Benny at Flannigan's Pub a couple days ago. Something's going on with those two, but I don't know what."

"Agreed. I talked to Nelson Rockwell. He said that after he accused Ariana of stealing his jewelry, someone slashed his tires. He thinks it was Benny. That's what they were arguing about at the Precious Gems and Jewelry Fair. I'm starting to think Benny could be behind the string of thefts all over town. He only seems to be targeting businesses. That is right up Benny's alley." Nik looked out at the yard and wrinkled his forehead.

Wolfgang whined louder.

"What is wrong with him?" I asked. "He hasn't even bothered with Prissy's taunting. That's not like him."

"I know. He's been acting funny for a couple days. I thought maybe he was bored, so I took him to Dino's Doggie Daycare today. They said he whined the whole time and didn't act like his usual self. As soon as he got home, he headed straight out back."

I stood up. "Well, something is obviously wrong with him." I started walking down his steps and into his backyard. "Get down here with me, Detective. I still don't trust he won't be naughty and lick me again."

"Right behind you, Ballas," he said from close to my ear and a shiver zipped down my spine despite the heat.

Wolfgang ignored us both.

That was a first. "You need to mow your yard." I was a freak about ours and mowed the lawn in a perfect diagonal pattern when I had time. When I didn't, I hired a lawn service, but I never let it go. Nik's was uneven all over the place. "And pick up after your dog." I plugged my nose. "It reeks out here in the heat."

"I always pick up after Wolf. That smell isn't from him." Nik looked around his yard. "Wait, where's my pooper scooper?"

"Your what?"

"The big metal contraption I have for picking up a dog's droppings."

"Oh, that thing. I've seen you use it, but I don't see it anywhere back here. All I can say is thank goodness for cats and litter boxes." I shuddered at the thought of all those germs. Cats were so self-sufficient.

"Hmph. Ma must have moved it." He tried to take Wolf by the collar and move him, but the dog refused to budge. In fact, he moved closer to the fence. "What is up with you, boy?" Nik stepped closer to the fence and looked over the top, then froze.

"What's wrong?" Our yards backed up to woods.

"Found my pooper scooper."

"You did?" I ran over to the fence and peered over the top asking, "What on earth is it doing beyond the fence?"

No words were necessary.

The widow lay dead with the pooper scooper by her head.

"Dinner's ready," Nik's ma yelled through the kitchen window.

My eyes met Nik's and the message was clear as day.

Things had just gotten worse for Chloe Stevens, and I didn't think I would ever eat again.

CHAPTER 11

"Are you sure you don't remember anything else, Ms. Stevens?" Captain Crenshaw asked, sitting across from Chloe at the table in the interrogation room of Clearview Connecticut Police Station. He sat there in his tailored-to-perfection gray suit that made his eyes pop, looking distinguished as ever with his salt and pepper hair buzzed and edged precisely. His face was smooth shaven and expressionless.

You would never guess he had asked her out on a date just recently.

"Really, Quincy? We're back to Ms. Stevens? After all we've been through together?" Chloe looked at the captain with a hurt expression, but he couldn't quite meet her eyes. Or wouldn't. He was all business, when what she needed most was for him to believe she was innocent.

I patted her back, lending support however I could. *You haven't even called me to see how I'm doing. Guess all you wanted was...* I dropped my hand, feeling my cheeks heat, and not wanting to invade her privacy. I once again had to give my statement, having been one of the people to discover yet another dead body. I didn't know what was happening in Clearview lately, but I was over it. I was only allowed to stay because Chloe had asked for it, and Captain Crenshaw had allowed her that much at least.

Nik cleared his throat loudly, giving *Quincy* a look that spoke volumes.

Captain Crenshaw's face flushed a dark red. "Sorry, Chloe," he said quietly. "I need to distance myself during this investigation so there's no conflict of interest." His gaze shot to Nik's, then quickly looked away. "I hope you understand."

"I understand it's your loss, *Captain Crenshaw*." She straightened her spine. "I also understand you don't believe I'm innocent."

He let out a sigh, then went back to being all business. "I never said that, Ms. Stevens. I'm simply looking at the facts." He scanned his notebook. "You were the only one home during the day for the past couple of days. The coroner said Ms. Simone died of blunt force trauma to the head yesterday morning." He met her eyes. "You say you don't take sleeping pills, yet you're pretty much comatose during your naps to the point where you don't hear, see, or remember anything." He checked his notes again. "Your fingerprints were on the, uh, fecal removing device. Shall I go on?"

"I don't do drugs, Captain Crenshaw. And, of course, my fingerprints were on the pooper scooper. The least I can do to help my son out is clean up around his place for letting me stay there since *you* won't let me go home." She stabbed a finger in his direction, displaying her fiery Greek temper which also didn't help her case. "Shall *I* go on?"

I touched her arm in warning, then quickly pulled my hand away. Along with reading someone's mind came feeling all their emotions. Chloe Stevens had a mix of frustration, fury, and fear all battling each other to take over. She was going to need a good therapist when this was done.

Lucky for her I knew plenty.

"Look, Captain, Ma is a small woman," Nik said. "I'm not saying the widow was a big woman, but my ma wouldn't be able to carry her out behind my fence. There were no drag marks on the ground or anything. I think the real killer is trying to set my ma up. The question is, why?"

"I think Detective Stevens is right, Captain," Boomer said. He'd been sitting quietly at the end of the table, observing.

Nik shot him a look of appreciation. No matter who was on the case, they were partners and friends. Jaz had told me Boomer hated being caught in the middle between Nik and his captain, believing Detective Stevens should be allowed on his mother's case. Who else would be more vested in getting at the truth than him? In the meantime, Boomer was doing everything he could to help.

"Look into it, Matheson." The captain stared hard at Nik. "I still don't want you anywhere near this case, Stevens. Understood?"

"Understood, Sir."

"Any news on the Business Bandit?"

"Not since Nelson Rockwell's tires were slashed. The Bandit has been quiet for a few days. I'm waiting for him to slip up. He can't cover his tracks forever."

"That's a good point. Good work, Detective. Stay on it."

Nik nodded once and then stood. "If we're all done here, Captain, I'd like to take my ma home."

"Sure. She's free to go," Captain Crenshaw said. "Keep an eye on her, Detective. If someone's trying to frame your mother, they obviously mean her harm. I would hate to see anything bad happen."

Chloe harumphed. "*She* is right here, and *she* is no longer your concern." Nik's ma stood up, then left without another word, which was probably a good thing. Forget about the killer...

Chloe's thoughts were going to be the death of her yet.

~

LATER THAT DAY, when I knew most of the people on Chloe's street would still be at work, I took advantage of the vacant houses to do a little snooping of my own. Maybe the police missed something at the crime scene. They'd certainly had enough time for the CSI unit to sweep the house from top to bottom, so I wasn't worried about disturbing anything.

A nagging feeling in my gut wouldn't go away. My gut had always steered me right. I just couldn't understand why Ariana would go to Chloe's house that late at night. Why would someone drug Chloe unless they didn't want her to discover the real reason they were there. Maybe Ariana surprised them, so they killed her to shut her up and make it look like it was Chloe. But what could they have been after? And that still didn't answer what Ariana was doing there so late to begin with.

Then there was Nina Simone. She'd threatened Chloe to stay away from the captain, then she disappeared for a few days, only to wind up dead behind Nik's fence. Why was she at his house to begin with unless to confront Chloe again? And even more confusing, why was the killer there? Did Nina see the real killer, so the killer took her out to shut her up as well?

Once again, they had made it look like Chloe did it. I was beginning to think the captain was right.

Chloe Stevens could be in real danger.

There were still too many questions unanswered, and we were running out of time.

Glancing around the block, my theory had been correct and everyone's cars were gone. Good. I'd parked my Prius down the street and cut around to Chloe's back yard, so no one's door cameras would have me on video. I froze for a moment, chill bumps sprinkling over my arms, as the sensation of being watched made my hair fill with static electricity. I hoped my skin cells and hair follicles wouldn't be permanently damaged after this.

Pushing those terrifying thoughts aside, I reasoned that my overactive imagination was having fun at my expense. *Again*. Squaring my shoulders, I continued on my way until I stepped through the trees into Chloe's backyard.

I had to agree with my cousin Yanni. Erik really had done a fabulous job on Chloe's back yard. The shrubs and flowers along the stone walkway were blooming beautifully, the marble statues were tastefully placed around the grounds—which I hadn't thought possible—with the gazebo being the centerpiece. Leave it to Yanni to have Erik continue to mow the lawn and pull the weeds while Chloe was away. My cousin was nothing if not professional. I was proud of how far he'd taken his business. He even handled the local businesses as well.

Pulling on my sterile, clear latex gloves, I ducked under the crime scene tape. I fished the spare key out of its hiding place beneath Zeus's foot—same as my family's—and let myself in the back door. Shaking my head, I had to chuckle. If they all hid their spare keys in the same place, who did they think they were keeping out since most of the town was Greek?

Focusing back to the task at hand, I let my eyes adjust to the inside of the house. I'd purposely chosen daytime, so I wouldn't have to turn my phone light on. The sky was overcast, calling for rain, making the rooms darker than normal. Chloe's house was a cute three-bedroom ranch. The front door opened into the foyer and living room, with the kitchen in the back of the house and the bedrooms off to the sides.

Thalia had seen Ariana enter through the front door after midnight, but her body was discovered by Chloe in the kitchen by the back door. I had a moment of PTSD over the thought of entering the kitchen again. Seeing a dead body, let alone two, wasn't something I would forget easily. Shaking off my nerves, I focused on the kitchen since that was where the murder had happened.

Squelching the need to sanitize first, I searched every inch of the space but didn't find a single thing. I continued on through the living room and guest bedrooms. Finally, I came to Chloe's bedroom. The end table by her bed still had sticky residue in a perfect circle from the glass she'd drank her Ouzo from. She must have brought her last glass to bed with her. The glass had been bagged and sent to the crime lab where they'd found the liquid laced with sedatives.

The same ones that had been inside the bottle.

Careful not to mess anything up, I got down on my hands and knees and searched all over but didn't see anything unusual. A crack of thunder sounded outside. Great. The storm had hit early. I was going to get soaked heading back to my Prius. I stood back up and started to leave. Having no choice, I turned on my phone light to see. A flash caught my eye. I moved my phone around, and saw the flash again.

Bending down, I held my phone closer to the register and could just make out what looked like a diamond earring beneath the heat vent. I pulled out the register, snagged the earring with my gloved hand, then put the register back in place. Slipping the earring deep in my short's pocket, I stood up and started to turn around when a searing pain shot through my head and the world around me went black.

~

"KALLI, WAKE UP," a rough voice said from somewhere above me as an equally rough hand patted my cheek. *You'd better be okay for both our sakes.*

That had me opening my eyes. "Erik? What are you doing here?"

"I could ask you the same thing." Relief flashed over his face. "I was covering some of Ms. Stevens' rose bushes before the storm when I noticed her back door had blown open. I went to close it, and I heard someone inside. I thought someone was robbing the place. Imagine my surprise when I found you on the floor in her bedroom of all places."

I raised a hand to my head. "Ouch." A massive welt was forming.

"Can you sit up?" he asked.

"Let me try." I struggled to move.

He reached out his hand to help.

"No, please, don't touch me."

He froze with wide eyes.

"Sorry, I don't like to be touched." And right now, my brain couldn't handle any more bombarding. I gingerly sat up and felt nauseas as I held my head together. It felt like it was going to fall apart. "Oh, boy. I think I have a concussion."

"Your cousin is not going to be happy with me," he muttered.

"Forget about my cousin. Detective Stevens is going to be furious with *me*." I looked at Erik and chewed my bottom lip. "I won't tell if you don't."

"I don't know about that, Ms. Ballas. You need to see a doctor."

"And I will, I promise." I slowly got to my feet and walked back to the kitchen, looking around as I went. "Did you see anyone or anything that might have hit me?"

He shook his head as he reached my side. "Not a thing. I heard a noise, came in to see where it was coming from, and saw you. That's it. I must have scared off whoever it was. I'm just glad for the storm; otherwise, I wouldn't have come by until tomorrow morning to tend to the yard."

"You and me both."

"What were you doing here, anyway?" He eyed me curiously.

"I wanted to surprise Chloe with the book I'd seen her reading before the murder to take her mind off her situation, but I didn't find it." I made that story up as my cover because my cousins were even worse than Detective Dreamy when it came to keeping me safe. None of them would let me out of their sight if they found out someone, most likely the killer, had tried to stop me from discovering the truth.

We walked out back through the pouring rain and ducked beneath the gazebo.

Erik stood there, deep in thought for a moment, then seemed to make up his mind about something. "Alright, Ms. Ballas, I won't tell anyone I saw you here, but please don't put me in this situation again. Not to mention there's still a killer on the loose, and this string of robberies going on is no joke. I wouldn't want to see you put yourself in any more danger."

You and the rest of the men in my life, I thought, but said, "No worries. I will definitely be more careful in the future. And I will tell Detective Stevens eventually."

"Tell me what?" came a honey-smooth voice from the shadows.

I groaned, dreading what was coming. "Erik Thompson, meet my friend, Detective Stevens," I said.

Nik emerged from the shadows and joined us beneath the gazebo. Unlike us, he had an umbrella. *Smart man.* He studied Erik for a moment. "I thought you looked familiar. Nice to officially meet you. My ma can't stop raving about the work you did on her yard. It's much appreciated.

Erik nodded once to Nik, looking uncomfortable. He really didn't handle praise well. "Just doin' my job, same as now."

"Thank God you were by the looks of it." Nik studied me closer. "Is that blood on your head, Ballas?"

I reached a hand up to my head and touched the bump. Letting out a little yelp, I pulled my hand away and it was bloody. I could feel my face drain of color as I swayed on my feet. Nik dropped his umbrella and caught me.

"I'll take it from here, Thompson." Nik lifted me into his arms. "Thank you for what you did."

"My pleasure." Erik fished a hat out of his back pocket and pulled it onto his head before disappearing into the rain.

"I'm guessing this is what you didn't want to tell

me," Nik said close to my ear as he carried me in the other direction toward the street. *Why can't you listen and keep your nose out of places it doesn't belong?*

"You should talk. Your nose isn't supposed to be here, either."

He looked down at me in confusion. "What? I said, I'm guessing this is what you didn't want to tell me." He frowned, eyeing my growing lump.

Whoops. "I mean, I know neither of us are supposed to be here, so what are you doing at your ma's house?"

"You weren't answering my calls, so I drove around looking for you. When I saw your Prius parked down the street, I got suspicious. Turns out I was right to think you were up to something. How did you hit your head?"

"I didn't. Someone hit it for me."

Nik stopped walking. "What?" His voice lowered an octave, and I could feel his entire body tense. He cursed silently.

"Your ma wouldn't like you cussing."

"I didn't realize I did that out loud."

Double whoops. It was really hard to keep actual words and thoughts clear in my head right now. "I'm fine. Erik scared the culprit off."

"The culprit could have been the killer, Kalli. This isn't a game. You could have been killed." He started walking again, holding me tighter. *I couldn't handle it if you were taken from me.*

"Aw that's sweet." *Shoot.* I kept talking, hoping he would ignore my earlier words. "My head hurts so bad. It was worth it, though, because I found something." I struggled in his arms and pulled out the earring from my shorts.

"Who's is that?"

"Not your ma's. She told me she refused to wear diamonds since her divorce. The house is brand new. Ariana was murdered in the kitchen and she had on different earrings. This is a single diamond stud, and it was in the register of your ma's bedroom. I'm thinking it was the real killer's earring, but what was it doing in the bedroom. And what woman has a diamond stud like this one?"

"Or man." Detective Stevens narrowed his eyes. "Benny wears a diamond earring about that size."

"We should have Nelson Rockwell look at it. We can't let Crabby Crenshaw know we found it. He'll lock us up and throw away the key for sure."

"I'll give it to Detective Matheson to turn in as evidence. He owes me." Nik walked past my car.

"Hey, wait. Where are you taking me?"

"Straight to the hospital." *There's more than a bump going on in that pretty head of hers. I think her brains have been scrambled.*

If he only knew.

CHAPTER 12

"You sure did it this time, Kalli," Doc LaLone said.

He was in his sixties with thick white hair and kind, light blue eyes. He still wore a white lab coat with a stethoscope around his neck, old school style, but I didn't trust any other doctor. I'd never seen anyone else since my parents adopted me at birth. He knew all about my quirks and was careful to only touch me when he had to. Unlike most people, I actually liked the smell of antiseptic because it reassured me things were clean.

Nik grunted. "I knew this was going to happen, but she never listens."

Nik sat in a padded chair in the corner of the country-blue painted room with pictures of Doc's children and grandchildren scattered around the counter. The walls were filled with drawings and pictures sent in from all of his patients over the years. There were a couple other doctors around town, but Doc LaLone was by far the favorite.

"Is it bad? Am I dying?" I twisted my hands in my

lap, my clothes still damp from the downpour. What the heck was happening to me?

"You'll live, Ms. Kalliope Mary Ballas, but you have one heck of a concussion." He gave me the same stern look I'd seen many times growing up under his medical care. "I want you to take it easy for the next six weeks. No arguments. You can't afford to be stubborn this time. Your brain isn't anything to mess around with."

"Okay, I promise." That earned me another grunt from Detective Serious Pants Stevens. I ignored him and lowered my voice. "By the way, Doc, did the rest of my brain seem okay? Like you didn't see anything else unusual, did you?" I held my breath.

"From anyone else, I might think that's a strange question." He chuckled. "Let me ease your fears. You're perfectly healthy, and your brain looks just fine. So please take better care of it, okay?"

"Okay, good." I breathed out a sigh of relief. Maybe it was just my imagination running away with me again. "I will, I promise."

"Now tell me what *really* happened." Doc studied me, then his gaze settled on Nik's. "No fall, no matter how hard, could have given her a lump like that. Someone hit her over the head, didn't they?"

"It's taken care of, Doc. You have my word."

Doc nodded. "How's your mother doing? Is she sleeping okay? If she needs a refill on those sedatives, just let me know."

"Ma swears she never took them. She thinks someone drugged her, and I have to say I'm starting to think that might be true. Especially after the bottle of Ouzo was found laced with the same sedative."

"Hmmm. She's not the only one in town I've prescribed those same sedatives to." Doc seemed to realize he'd spoken out loud. "Now, you know, with HIPAA laws I can't tell you who. Just know there's more of those pills around town."

"Thanks, Doc." Nik stood and helped me off the exam table.

A few minutes later, we were on our way home. The storm had let up, and the sky was clear once more. We didn't talk the whole way because Nik still wasn't happy with me for going rogue on him after we'd made a deal to work together. As we turned onto our street, we both let out a moan. There wasn't a single place to park since the Ballas and Pagonis families were everywhere.

"I can't believe they didn't leave us a spot in our own driveway." I held my head as it started pounding harder.

"I can." Nik parked the car way down the street, and we climbed out.

We hadn't made it twenty feet before news that we were home zipped through the family grapevine. My ma came running down the street, her arms outstretched and waving wildly like the inflatable tube man sign, followed closely by Aunt Tasoula who was fanning her face at Mach speed.

I held my hands out in front of me in a stay command like I would if I were trying to stop a pack of wild dogs. I just didn't want them to jar my head and hurt my brain any more than it already was.

They skidded to a halt, out of breath as they gaped at me.

"Speak to me, Kalliope Mary Ballas," Ma yelled at the top of her lungs. "Test one, two, three. Can you hear me?"

I waved my hands to get her to stop shouting as I slowly nodded, holding my head with both hands.

"Oh, woe is me, she's got a broken tongue," Aunt Tasoula wailed. "I've seen this before. YiaYia's great, great YiaYia had this before. She couldn't talk for a year. It's no good. She's ruined."

"I can talk just fine."

"It's a miracle." Ma's hands formed a prayer position. "She's cured."

"Praise be to the gods." Aunt Tasoula made the sign of the cross.

"Yes, it's a miracle I'm still standing after all this," I muttered.

"Let's get you home. I'll make a pot of tea with aloe. That will help your head." Ma hustled along beside me but kept her hands to herself, thank goodness.

"What is happening to our town?" Pop paced the driveway. "First that poor child was murdered, then that poor widow was murdered, and now my very own daughter almost died. Someone has put a curse on Clearview, I tell you."

"Something has to be done to stop this madness, I say." Papou Homer shook his head, standing with his arms crossed and watching my father pace, while YiaYia chased Frona around the yard.

Thalia and Eleni sat on the front steps. "I could ask my boyfriend's sister, Marigold, to use her voodoo magic," Eleni said.

"Have her use it on Benny Balboa," Thalia said. "The man's a snake. I still think he's behind either the murders or the thefts or both. He's involved somehow. I just know it. Poor Aunt Chloe is having a fit of the vapors over this whole mess."

"Okay, I'll text her now." Eleni pulled out her phone.

"I tried to warn Nina Simone about dealing with

Benny," Thalia said, "but she wouldn't listen and look what happened to her."

"Dealing with Benny? What do you mean?" Nik asked. "Do you know what kind of deal they were making?"

"She said something about selling her late husband's jewelry to him. That Rockwell Jewelers said they weren't worth anything."

"Interesting," Nik said, and I could see him making mental notes.

"Sure, Benny will give her money for them, if she's into drug money. The question is why would he want them if they're not worth anything? I told her as much, but again, she didn't listen. And now she's dead." Thalia shuddered. "I dodged a bullet when Ariana stole Benny from me. I don't want to be linked in any way imaginable to the mob. Once they sink their claws into you, they don't let go."

As interesting as the conversation was, I felt like I was about to pass out. "Well, everyone can see that I'm fine. So, I'd like to go inside now." I walked through the front door and shooed even more family members out.

Nik took one look at me and followed suit, getting rid of everyone else who lingered. He joined me a few minutes later on my couch, and we both took a moment to breathe a sigh of relief. "How are you, really?"

"I'm okay. I just need quiet." It felt nice, just the two of us, sitting in silence. The silence didn't last long as ten minutes later the doorbell rang once more.

Nik started to get up, but I motioned him back down.

"This is my half of the house. I'll get it." I opened the door to a man I didn't recognize. "May I help you?"

"I'm Detective Johnson, here to see Detective

Stevens." A man who was larger than life and looked like he'd just come from a wrestling ring in Hawaii stood before me dressed all in black with dark sunglasses.

Nik appeared from behind me. "Darnell?" His face broke out into a huge grin. "I've never been happier to see someone, buddy." He threw his arms in a bear hug around the giant, who hugged him back.

"I wish it was under better circumstances." The man's face grew grim as he pulled off his sunglasses.

"What do you mean?"

"Gabe Scarlatta escaped from prison three months ago."

~

"There you go, Darnell." Chloe set a mountain of food in front of the giant, fully relaxed in her element of cooking and caring for people.

I was grateful not to have to worry about cooking dinner. I'd fed Prissy, and just wanted to sleep, but Nik wouldn't let me. Said it wasn't good to sleep just yet. He insisted on not letting me out of his sight because of the concussion.

"Thanks, Ms. Stevens. I appreciate it." Darnell took a bite and smiled as he chewed. "It's delicious, just like I remember."

Darnell had been Nik's former partner from back in the city for a decade, and his best friend for longer than that. Their mothers had grown close during that time when Darnell's father, who was a lawyer, had helped Chloe with her divorce.

"How's your mother?" Chloe asked.

"She's good. Missing you since you moved."

"You tell her to come visit any time." Her face pinched. "Well, after this whole mess is over, anyway."

Nik and I sat at the table in his kitchen while Chloe bustled about, making all sorts of dishes. Ever since the widow was discovered dead out behind the fence, she was paranoid that she would be next.

"Did you lock the door when you came in, Nikos?"

"Yes, Ma. You're safe here. I had all the locks changed and put in security cameras, plus Captain has a car patrolling the area both night and day."

"Good. You kids catch up. I'm going to sit a spell." She shivered, then carried her tea to the living room.

I was nursing a cup of tea as well, not having much of an appetite after getting my skull cracked. I had to admit I was feeling a little nervous myself. I kept having that same sensation of being watched.

"I see you've got a new partner to keep you on your toes." Darnell shot me a wink as he grinned wide. "You need it."

"She's much better to look at than your ugly mug." Nik laughed, then his smile slipped a little. "But she's not my partner. Just my neighbor."

"And friend," I added. "But I agree, Detective Johnson. He does need someone to keep him on his toes and keep him from getting himself and his ma into trouble by sticking his nose where it doesn't belong."

"I'm not the one who got whacked over the head."

I winced and touched my head, feeling the pain of getting hit all over again. "I was just trying to find a book for your ma." I couldn't quite meet his eyes.

"Right. I have plenty of books around here for my ma to read."

"You read?" Darnell coughed.

"Tell me more about Scarlatta escaping," Nik changed the subject. "He was in a United States federal prison. I thought escaping from those would be pretty much impossible with today's technology."

"They were transporting him to a different prison. You busted him for nearly killing his wife and daughter. A lot of inmates are husbands and fathers and don't like a guy like that. Let's just say his life has been a living hell for the last five years. Guess the technology's not so good in the transport system." Darnell set his fork down and wiped his mouth, having finished the mountain of food. "The Feds are on the case now that he's a fugitive. I had some time to take off and wanted to give you a head's up that he's out. And, well, I wanted to see for myself how you and your ma were doing with everything that's going on here. Offer my two cents and see if I could help."

"Thanks, man. It's been frustrating. Captain put me on a robbery case, actually, a string of robberies that have been happening around town. Detective Matheson is on the murder cases. Captain Crenshaw says I'm too close, yet ironically, I just found out he dated my ma. I'd say that makes him closer than me."

Darnell's dark eyebrow crooked up. "I don't imagine you're too happy about that bombshell."

Nik grunted. "Would you be?"

"I'd probably be in jail if my mom dated my captain, given my mother is still married to my father." Darnell rubbed his smooth jaw and wisely changed the subject. "You know, I heard about other towns around the area being hit with robberies in their businesses. I wonder if they're all related."

"Maybe." Nik wrote something down in his notes. "See what you can find out on your end, would you?"

"Sure thing. I'll let you know if anything turns up."

"While you're at it, see if your contacts know anything about recent mob activity. Benny's up to something."

"I heard he was in Clearview, and we both know from experience, wherever Benny is, trouble isn't far behind."

"Amen to that."

The door to Nik's house whipped open, sending Wolfgang into a barking frenzy. "It's just me, you crazy beast," Jaz said, fending off his slobbery kisses.

"Wolf sit," I said, and he plopped his fanny down immediately on a whine.

Jaz's eyes zeroed in on me, and she flew over to the table to wrap me in her arms. "Don't you scare me like that ever again." *I will kill you myself if you put yourself in that kind of danger again, missy. I know you can hear me.*

I patted her arm in answer, and she let go. "I'm fine, really. Just a little bruised. Don't worry. Detective Stubborn isn't letting me out of his sight."

"Well, he can take a break. You're coming home with me, and that's that." Jaz snagged a plate and filled it with Chloe's amazing food, then she blinked as she finally noticed Darnell. "Well, aren't you a handsome dude. Too bad I'm not single."

Darnell's skin darkened to a reddish brown, and his mouth fell slightly open as if he wanted to speak but lost his words.

Welcome to the spell of Jazlyn Alvarez, I thought, actually pitying the poor sap.

Detective Matheson chose that moment to grace us with his presence. He walked in, took one look at a besotted Darnell, then patted the man's shoulder. "I know that look. Been there, buddy. It'll pass." Boomer kissed Jaz on the top of her head, then sat down and filled a plate, digging in with gusto.

Jaz rolled her eyes, but her slight smile gave her away. She loved every minute of the attention she got. I envied her for how easy relationships were for her. My gaze was drawn to Detective Dreamy like it always was whenever he was near me, and his eyes softened as he looked at me. The traitorous butterflies began to dance in my stomach once more...until his cellphone rang.

What now? I really couldn't take any more surprises in one day.

"Detective Stevens," he answered, his face forming into a serious expression as he listened. "I'll be right there." He hung up.

Darnell and I both looked at him in question.

"There's been another robbery." His eyes met mine and held, the softness turning to intensity, and my butterflies turned into a knot of worry. "This time at your aunt Tasoula's salon."

CHAPTER 13

"What am I going to do?" Aunt Tasoula wailed. "They took my money, hair products, makeup...everything. I have nothing left."

"You have family." Ma hugged her hard.

"Ophelia's right, Tasoula." Pop paced the sidewalk in front of Hera's Halo while rubbing his hands together. "Greek's take care of their own. We will figure this out. Tell me what happened again?"

"I closed early when we heard about what happened to Kalli. After I saw with my own two eyes that she was okay, I took my grandson Christos and his father Adonis out to dinner at Rosalita's Place."

Ma gasped and stopped hugging her sister.

"What can I say?" Tasoula lifted her shoulders, waving her tissue around. "My grandson loves Mexican food."

"It's okay, Tasoula, ignore her. Keep going." Pop shushed my ma.

Ma gave him a glaring look that said, *It's not okay, but I will let it slide this time only because she has nothing now*, then she looked at her sister with pity. "You may continue with your story."

"Anyway," Aunt Tasoula continued, "when we were finished, I realized I forgot a mystery I was reading at my salon. All I wanted was to curl up and read a good book when I got home after the eventful day we've had." She looked at Ma and teared up again. "They even took my book, and I was at a really good part."

"Oh, Soula, I'm so sorry." Ma dropped the attitude and patted her sister's back with genuine affection.

Detective Stevens came outside the shop with Detective Matheson by his side while the crime scene investigators worked their magic inside. Hopefully this time the Business Bandit would make a mistake and leave a clue behind.

"Well, what do you think?" I asked Nik.

"There's no rhyme or reason with these thieves. The Bandit doesn't target only one type of business, and he doesn't just take money. He takes all sorts of goods. We can't even do a stake-out because there's no predicting which business he'll hit next. He's also very meticulous and neat. Not a smash and grab kind of perp."

"The Bandit is definitely a pro," Boomer added. "He must get the lay of the land first and know how to bypass security. There hasn't been any video footage taken. Alarms are never set off. He always strikes when no one is around."

"There has to be a way to stop him," Jaz said. "This is getting ridiculous. I don't feel safe at all, even with a detective for a boyfriend. I feel like I need to spend every night at my boutique just to protect my livelihood."

Boomer hugged her.

"All I know is this has been the longest day of my life." I touched my head gingerly and felt nauseous again.

"I'm taking you home." Jaz looped her arm through mine. *Testing one, two, three. Can you still hear me?*

I eased my arm out of hers and stepped away. "Loud and clear," I said, then rubbed my temples.

"What's loud and clear," Nik asked.

"Jaz's command that she's taking me home."

"Roger that." Boomer kissed Jaz's cheek. "I'll catch up with you later, Babe. I've got a few leads of my own I want to check out on the murder cases." Boomer looked at Nik. "Care to compare notes, Stevens?"

"I thought you'd never ask, Matheson." Nik looked at me and winked. "Later, Babe."

I rolled my eyes, but couldn't deny the little thrill that ran through me.

~

THE NEXT MORNING, I felt much better. My head still hurt, but I wasn't nauseous anymore. I set Prissy down and gave her one final stroke across her silky fur. She must have sensed I'd needed some tender loving care because she'd curled up in my lap this morning while I sipped my tea. Triple checking the house was secure, I headed out my front door and checked the lock three times. Satisfied, I walked next door and knocked.

The door swung open. "Hang on just a second while I grab my purse." Chloe disappeared.

Nik's car wasn't in the driveway, so he must be gone to work already. I pushed down my disappointment and smiled when Chloe reappeared.

"Ready?" I asked.

"As I'll ever be."

We slipped into my Prius, and I headed downtown.

"Can you turn the air on, dear? It's a bit stuffy in here." Chloe fanned her flushed cheeks.

"I can roll the windows down." Air conditioning used recycled air. Clearview didn't have many air pollutants to worry about like some big cities, and at least outside air was fresh. Lord only knew what the germs from recycled air would do to my insides. I shuddered.

I rolled down the window and did a double-take.

Chloe had stuck her head out the window like Wolfgang. "That's better. Thank you, dear." Her cheeks still looked a little red.

"Are you okay?"

"Just nervous, I guess. I've never had my great, great grandma's necklace appraised before."

"Does it really matter if it's worth much? I would think the sentimental value behind it is irreplaceable."

"You're right. I'm just always afraid of losing it. I guess if I knew it was worth a lot of money, I would be even more of a mess."

I pulled alongside the curb in a parking spot right out front. "Well, we're about to find out."

We climbed out of the car, and I locked it before we headed inside.

Rex was in full uniform with his mailbag slung across his body. He smiled and waved at Chloe, then his smile faded when his eyes met mine. He tipped his hat, then cleared his throat before saying, "Have a nice day, Ladies," then he slipped quickly out the door and down the street.

I wished he would stop being so nervous around me. Just because I designed sexy lingerie and had seen him at the Singles Club, he'd been a bundle of nerves around me ever since.

Focus on one problem at a time, Kalli, I told myself.

Nelson stood behind the counter helping Eleanor

and Olivia Bennet with new watches, while Lois Flannigan was at another counter looking at anniversary rings. They all glanced up when Chloe and I walked through the front door.

"Yay, you took our advice." Eleanor clapped.

"You should see the great finds Nelson has this week." Olivia smiled wide at Nelson, and his cheeks turned pink. "You'd better amp up your security with these fabulous finds lying around."

"Don't you worry. I've doubled the security I had before. More cameras inside and out and a secret alarm." His face hardened. "That Bandit's not gonna get anything else that belongs to me."

"Good for you, Nelson. Luckily the pub hasn't been hit yet." Lois shivered, then looked at us with excitement in her eyes. "The girls and I come here every week to see what new items have come in." Lois pointed at the counter in front of her. "My twentieth wedding anniversary is coming up this year, and this ring has my name all over it."

"Just gotta convince Mr. Flannigan of that," Nelson added.

"Oh, don't you worry. I have my ways of convincing my man to do pretty much anything I want." She giggled like a woman half her age as the Bennet sisters joined her to see the ring she had pointed at.

"What brings you to my store today, ladies?" Nelson focused on me. "Are we browsing engagement rings?"

My stomach flipped. "Oh, no, no, no. Not me. I'm just here with Chloe—er—Ms. Stevens. To lend support as a friend, that is. Not as anything to do with her son." I pointed to Chloe. "The floor's all hers." Good lord, what was my problem?

"Well, I have this heirloom necklace. It's been in

my family for over a century. I've never had it appraised. I have to admit, I've always been curious as to how much it might be worth." She handed the necklace to Nelson, who brought it over to another counter with tools, a magnifying glass, and a bright light.

I hadn't really looked closely at the piece. It was stunning. A cameo of Aphrodite was carved into Sardonyx and surrounded by pearls, dazzling gems, and semi-precious stones that all looked genuine and very old. Olive leaves traveled up both sides of the chain delicately, growing smaller as they reached the top.

Nelson saw me staring at the necklace with my mouth agape, and he grinned slightly. "I have to agree, Ms. Ballas. The piece is fascinating. After Alexander the Great conquered the Persian empire, the Hellenistic period of jewelry was heavily influenced. Jewelry like this indicated a person's social status, power, and wealth. Many people during that time wore the jewelry to protect themselves and ward off evil."

"Oh, well, maybe I should wear it more often instead of hiding it away," Chloe said, adding, "Lord knows I've seen enough evil as of late."

"I heard." He shook his head. "This whole town hasn't been the same since that woman and her mother arrived to stir up trouble."

"I don't care much for either of them, but I have made my peace with Penelope. No mama should have to go through what she has been through." Chloe made the sign of the cross. "I think Ariana's ex-boyfriend is the real culprit of the evil in this town. I don't trust him one bit. He used to be connected to the mob, after all."

"You don't have to tell me. I'm with you on that," Nelson agreed with her. "I know he had something to do with my jewelry being stolen. I wouldn't be surprised if he's not the Bandit. That girl tried to pawn her fakes off on me. As if I can't tell the difference between a knock-off and the real deal."

"Detective Steven's cousin, Thalia, said something about Benny Balboa buying the widow, Nina Simone's, late husband's jewelry before she was murdered. Said she offered the jewelry to you first. Do you know anything about that?" I asked, watching the jewelry store owner closely for any reaction to my words.

"Yes, she came to my shop and tried to sell them to me. I felt bad because I think she was hurting for money. I don't think she and her husband had planned very well for their retirement, and his unexpected death in the line of duty caught her by surprise. I think that's why she kept trying to find a man to take care of her, the poor thing. Anyway, no matter how bad I felt for her, I'm a businessman first and foremost. That jewelry wasn't worth much." Nelson drew his brows together. "That's why it didn't make sense for Benny to buy them from her. What could he possibly want with useless jewelry?"

"I don't know, but Thalia tried to warn her to stay away from Benny. Nina didn't listen, and now she's dead." Chloe shook her head. "Another woman gone way too soon. I fear for the rest of us in town. When will it end? Who's next?"

"Maybe your niece, Thalia," Nelson said.

Chloe's hand flew to her chest as she sucked in a breath, her face draining of color. "Why would you say that?"

"Because just yesterday I had a meeting with a client for a unique piece I'm designing for him. We met at a restaurant on the outskirts of town for privacy. I was stunned to see Thalia in a corner booth with Benny."

"Why on earth would she have anything to do with that monster?" Her face turned crimson, and I could have sworn I saw steam escaping her ears. "I'm shocked because she always talks about how much she hates him." Chloe started hyperventilating, and I snatched a flyer off Nelson's desk and fanned her face. "Wait until I tell her mama," she managed to get out on a wheeze.

Nelson grabbed a paper bag from behind his counter and handed it to her. She breathed slow and deep as he continued. "I would have said something to her, but like I said, I was with a private client. The last thing I wanted to do was cause a scene. Then they left before we were finished."

The lump on my head throbbed suddenly, and I had the same feeling of being watched. I looked around the jewelry store and then out the window facing the street. Milly Donovan's eyes met mine as she stood outside the window display with four dogs on leashes. She stared for a moment longer, then looked away and kept walking.

"Maybe I should take Ms. Stevens home now," I said, keeping my eye on Milly as she hustled down the street, pondering what that was all about.

"May I keep your necklace for a few days?" Nelson asked Chloe. "I'd like to have a second set of eyes on this remarkable piece, but I'm pretty confident you're looking at six figures here."

My head whipped back and I dropped my purse. "As in one hundred thousand dollars?" I squeaked, picking it back up.

"No, Ms. Ballas." His gaze met mine and held. "As in close to a million."

The paper bag Chloe held popped, and she promptly fainted flat on her back.

CHAPTER 14

Doc LaLone stared into Chloe's eyes, watching her pupils as he shined a light in different directions. She sat on the same exam table I had not too long ago. He ran her through a series of tests I recognized well, and then looked at me with a raised brow as I sat in the same chair Nik had, probably feeling the same way I did right now.

I shrugged and lifted my hands palms up.

"What am I going to do with you both?" He wrote something in Chloe's chart, then he leveled a no-nonsense look at me. "I get the feeling you are not taking my advice seriously. You are supposed to be taking it easy and staying out of trouble, not running around playing cops and robbers."

"I swear I wasn't investigating anything. I was only shopping while Chloe was getting her family heirloom necklace appraised. Who would have expected that to be a dangerous activity?"

"I've seen my wife during a sale." He looked at us both with wary eyes. "I know how crazy you women can be."

"Oh, I hear you, Doc, but this wasn't about any sale." I slowly shook my head, still in shock over the news we'd heard. "I nearly fainted myself."

"I never imagined in my wildest dreams that my necklace would be worth a fortune." Chloe fanned her face. "I'm lucky I didn't have a heart attack."

"No, but now you have a concussion as well. Not as bad as Kalli's, but still one to take seriously. You only get one brain in this life, ladies. Maybe I need to outfit you both with helmets while in public."

"And ruin my hair?" Chloe patted her perfectly styled cut, looking at him with wary eyes now. "I don't think so, Doc."

"Beauty before common sense. That sounds about right with you women." He chuckled, then grew serious. "I was only half-kidding about the helmet, but you do have to be more careful." His eyes met mine. "You both do. Your brain can only take so much. If you keep abusing it, you could end up with permanent damage."

I suddenly wondered if my gift was damaging my brain every time I read someone's mind. How much stress could my brain take?

"Are you okay, Kalli? You look a little pale," Chloe asked, staring at me with worry-filled eyes.

"I'm fine, but I think Doc is right." I stood up and grabbed my purse. "We both could use some rest."

"I couldn't agree more. Finally, you're making sense," Nik said from the open door to the exam room. "Thanks for calling me, Doc. Joan said it was okay for me to come back here." Joan was Doc's wife who was also his nurse, and their daughter Cindy was his receptionist in their small family practice.

"I told her to send you back. These two need

babysitters, as you can see. I don't want either of them driving for the rest of the day."

"Hey, I'm not the one who fell," I said.

Doc reached out and took my wrist in his hand, staring at his watch and counting. He dropped my arm. "Just as I suspected. Your pulse is too fast. You might not have fallen, but this event definitely affected you."

"Don't worry, Doc. I've got this." Nik gave us both a stern look. "I'm putting them both on house arrest."

I gasped. "Under who's authority?"

"Mine."

Ten minutes later we were on our way back home.

"What about my car?"

"I already sent an officer to drive it home."

Out of options, I sulked in the backseat silently.

"The whole town is buzzing over the jewelry store incident," Nik finally said, glancing in the rear-view mirror at me with a frustrated expression then over to his ma. "What you were thinking, Ma?"

"What, I've always been curious about how much our family heirloom was worth. There's no harm in that."

"Are you kidding? There's still a murderer on the loose and a Bandit wreaking havoc on our town. You just put yourself and Kalli by association in a great deal of danger. That kind of money is enough to make even family members turn on each other to get their hands on that necklace."

"Well, you don't have to worry. I don't even have it."

Nik swerved and nearly went off the road. Jerking the car back between the white lines, he kept his eyes straight ahead and focused. "Ma, where is the necklace?"

"Nelson Rockwell has it. He asked if he could keep it for a couple days to verify his appraisal."

"And you let him? He's already been hit once by the Bandit."

"I'm not worried. He doubled his security."

"The Bandit is no amateur."

"Stop worrying, Nikos. Everything will be fine."

"Well, I'm doubling *my* security. People don't know you don't have the necklace on you. There's no telling the lengths they'll go to for something as valuable as that. I wish you'd left it in the safe where it belongs."

"Nelson Rockwell told us he saw Thalia having lunch with Benny Balboa at a remote restaurant on the outskirts of town when he was with a client," I said, more than ready to change the subject.

Nik nearly went off the road for a second time.

The thought of having that heirloom around and the possibility of being in danger was giving me major anxiety. I practiced my deep breathing and tried to relax, but Detective Dreamy's driving was making that impossible.

"Wait, did I hear you right?" Nik gripped the steering wheel, keeping his gaze trained on the road.

"That's what he said, and he has no reason to lie. He hates Benny, and he's worried the same fate as Ariana and the widow Simone will fall on Thalia. I don't get it. Your cousin made it clear she can't stand Benny, so why would she have lunch with him?"

"I don't know, but you can bet I'm going to find out."

"Speaking of finding things out." I watched him through the mirror. "Do you have any updates on the murder cases?"

"Actually, yes. Detective Matheson said when they

searched Nina Simone's house, they found the same sleeping pills Doc prescribed Ma by her bed."

"You know, I was supposed to go on my first date with the captain that night," Chloe chimed in. "But after my run in with Ariana and Penelope at the grocery store, I wasn't in the mood. Nina was in the liquor store when I bought the bottle of Ouzo. I'm not proud of myself, but I have to admit I made sure she knew about my date. Do you think she drugged me to make me fall asleep and ruin my date?"

"Maybe Ariana caught the widow in the act so she killed her in a moment of panic and then fled," I offered my two cents.

"Maybe, but then everyone knows Ma isn't dating anyone with the murder investigation going on. So why try to approach her at my house? And who killed Nina?"

"That's true," I agreed. "Besides, I don't think the diamond earring was hers, either. Nelson said she tried to sell her late husband's jewelry which wasn't worth much because she was hurting for money. I doubt she would have bought diamond earrings."

"All these questions are making my head hurt and making me stress out even more." Chloe pinched the bridge of her nose.

"I couldn't agree more." I nodded as Nik pulled into our driveway.

"Good because both of you need to relax. Doctor's orders, remember?"

I remembered, all right. And I had the perfect solution in mind.

~

NIK LEFT to follow up on some leads about the Business Bandit, while I asked my Aunt Tasoula to bring the girls for an emergency house call. The town had come together and donated all sorts of supplies to hold her over until her new shipment came in. Clearview was like that. Everyone always looked out for each other.

"Where is she," Aunt Tasoula asked when she arrived a few minutes later.

I pointed to the living room of my house. I didn't want Wolfgang disrupting our spa afternoon with all his germ-filled saliva love. I could hear his whining through the walls. He hadn't stopped whining since I'd taken his sweet YiaYia Chloe from him. He was getting a little too used to her always being around. I was afraid how he would be once she went back to her own place.

He's not your problem, Kalli. Remember, you and Nik are just friends. Just like you wanted. I sighed. To be honest, I didn't know what I wanted anymore. Except for some answers. I definitely wanted those, and I was determined to get them.

"Oh, you poor thing," my aunt said to Chloe. "My girls will pamper you today with a manicure and a pedicure."

"Aw, that's so sweet. You don't have to go to all that trouble," Chloe said, then sank a little deeper into the couch, holding her head as if it were about to fall off. Just moments ago, she'd been sitting up straight, reading a book.

"Girls, hurry. Chop-chop." Tasoula clapped her hands twice. "Grab the aloe. She's fading fast. She needs some TLC stat."

I bit back a giggle. I could tell Chloe was loving every minute of it, and well, my aunt loved to be involved in everything and feel needed. My ma was going to have a fit when she heard about this because she was stuck at work.

The doorbell rang, and I slipped out of the room to answer it. I looked through the peephole and smiled as I opened the door. "Thalia, I'm so glad you could come. Your aunt mentioned you, so I thought you should know."

Chloe *had* mentioned Thalia. That much was true. I would just let Thalia assume her aunt wanted to see her, when I suspected she really wanted to throttle her.

"I was so worried when I found out what happened." Thalia stepped through the front door and looked around. "Where is she?"

"Follow me." I led the way to our living room. Prissy hissed then went out on the deck through the sliding door I left partially open for her. She wasn't liking strangers intruding on our sanctuary. If I were being honest, I felt the need to follow them with a can of Lysol, but I forced myself to control the urge.

As soon as we walked into the room, Chloe Stevens spotted Thalia. She bolted up straight like I knew she would and thrust her finger in her niece's face. "Young lady, you have some explaining to do."

Thalia jerked to a stop, her eyes widening, then she pursed her lips. "I have some explaining to do? You're the one who fainted." She put her hands on her hips. "What the heck is going on, Aunt Chloe?"

"I can't blame her," Aunt Tasoula chimed in. "If I had a million-dollar necklace around my neck, I would have succumbed to a fit of the vapors for sure." She leaned closer to Chloe. "Are you royalty? Where is the necklace now? Can we see it?"

Everyone stopped moving and stared.

Chloe paused and her eyes met mine for a moment. Nik's words were going through both our minds by the look of it. That even family might do some crazy things when it came to that amount of money.

"It's in a safe place," she said vaguely. "It's too valuable to keep here. Make sure you spread that news around town."

"Oh, well, I understand that. Keep the desperados away. I'm sure what once was thought of as a blessing is now most definitely a curse." Tasoula made the sign of the cross. "You were wise to get rid of it."

"I didn't get rid of it. It's a family heirloom to go to my granddaughter one day. I just want it safe until all this craziness goes away." Chloe's eyes veered over to Thalia's. "And you, young lady, are the craziest one of all."

"Oh, my Zeus?" Tasoula and her girls all turned their attention on Thalia. "What did you do this time?"

"I didn't do anything," Thalia sputtered. "I came here to see if my aunt was okay because I thought you wanted to see me." Thalia's eyes turned suspicious as they settled on me then gave me a hard look.

I shrugged, playing the innocent card.

"You know what you did," Chloe said, drawing her attention once more. "Just wait until I tell your mama."

"Okay, but can you tell me first?" Thalia threw her hands up. "Because I really don't know what you're talking about."

"You had lunch with Benny Balboa." The room grew quiet as a tomb. "Care to tell us what *that* was about?"

I walked discreetly behind Thalia as she responded.

"I was warning him to stay away from the rest of

my family and friends, if you must know," she said, and I touched her shoulder and squeezed in support. *I hate him. I really don't want him to hurt anyone else I care about, but I have to finish this.*

Finish what?

I had no clue, but I had a feeling there was more to her story than she was letting on, and Detective Stevens wasn't going to like it.

CHAPTER 15

"Let me take Wolfgang for a walk," I said to Nik the next day. I'd had enough of house arrest, but had to admit he and Doc had been right. I did feel better today. "I think he's been missing Chloe since she's been spending more time at my place," I added. "I'll take him for a walk and then I'll drop him off at Dino's Doggy Daycare."

Detective Dreamy looked at me like I'd turned into a little green alien. "Are you sure you're feeling better today?"

"Wolf and I have a new understanding. He knows if he breaks my trust this time, there's no coming back from that." My eyes met Nik's, and his questioned if I was still talking about his dog or him. Admittedly, my words were probably for both. "Anyway, I feel bad for him. He's been such a good boy lately, and I've monopolized all of your ma's free time. This will give her a break, and do him some good."

"If you say so. Just so you know, he's a puller."

"Not with me."

Nik shook his head in defeat. "That's fine with me,

but don't say I didn't warn you. Deal?" He held out his hand.

"Deal." I shook his hand, and he held on longer than necessary. *I hate how things are between us. I just wish you'd give me a second chance.*

I let go of his hand, and for once, didn't have the urge to sanitize mine. I wasn't sure what that meant or how I was feeling. Actually, I knew exactly how I was feeling. I wanted to fling myself into his big strong arms and pick up where we left off, but another part of me was terrified to make myself that vulnerable. It was simply easier to make him think I wasn't ready because of his ex. According to him, they'd been over for a while before they broke up. He just hadn't wanted to hurt her.

He handed me Wolfgang's leash and said, "Good luck," before he walked out the door with a chuckle.

"All right, buddy, we're going to make your daddy eat his words." I looked Wolfgang in the eye. "You and I are going to be a team, right?" He cocked his massive head. "I'm doing you a favor, so don't you dare be naughty." He licked his lips. I eyed his tongue, gagged a little, and he quickly slipped it back inside as if he was the one who could read minds.

We'll see who has the last laugh.

Ten minutes later, we were at the dog shelter where Millie Donovan volunteered. I needed to know why she had been watching me through the window of Rockwell Jewelry Store. And even more curious was why she'd looked away guiltily when I caught her staring at me? What could I have possibly done to her?

I pulled in the parking lot and saw her car there. She walked the dogs from the shelter every morning. The shelter was at the end of Main Street, so she walked down the sidewalk past all the storefronts until she hit the park with a playground for children, a fenced in dog park for dogs, and a pavilion with picnic tables for events.

I climbed out of my Prius and started down the street, then ducked into an alleyway while I waited for Milly. Not long after, I heard Milly before I saw her. Yips and barks and howls from the happy canines she was walking.

"Remember, Wolf, behave yourself." I stepped out onto the curb and pretended to look in the window of the jewelry store.

I figured, why not meet her where the incident had happened. This was also where she had seen Nelson vow to get even with Ariana for trying to pawn fakes off on him. He believed she was the one behind stealing his jewelry, and then his tires were slashed, which was why he and Benny had argued at the community center. Because Nelson was positive Benny was the one behind it. Maybe Milly could answer a few questions for me.

I turned to look at her and feigned surprise. "Hi, Milly. So good to see you." I fell into step beside her. "Mind if I walk with you?"

Today she only had two mutts, which Wolf didn't seem to mind one bit. And he was on his best behavior, thank goodness. Nik was crazy. Wolf wasn't a puller. He was a perfect gentleman.

"Sure, I guess," Milly said, not quite meeting my eyes. She was a petite thing, with light red hair, pale green eyes, and freckles. She was soft spoken and had a natural, pure kind of pretty, probably in her midthirties.

We walked down the street in silence for a few

minutes, passing various stores and waving to people we both knew.

"I didn't think you liked dogs," she finally said. "I mean you have a cat, and I've just never seen you with a dog. Especially a big one like Wolfgang who slobbers. Doesn't that bother you with your..." Her eyes grew wide with horror. "I mean, I'm sorry, I—"

"It's okay. I'm sure everyone in town knows about my quirks. I'll admit I'm a germaphobe and have a little OCD, but it's getting better in some areas." Detective Dreamy's lips flashed before my eyes, and I blinked to refocus on the reason I was here. I continued talking. "I'm definitely more of a cat person, but Wolfgang is growing on me. He and I have an understanding. Don't we, Wolf." He let out a bark right on cue, and I patted his head.

"Oh, well, that's good." She fidgeted uncomfortably.

"Speaking of liking, did I do something wrong? I know we don't know each other that well, but it seems like lately you've been acting strange towards me."

Her face flushed crimson. "I'm sorry. It's not you. Well, I mean, it *is* you, but it's not your fault. You're so pretty, I'm sure lots of men like you."

"I'm confused." That was not the response I had been expecting. "What are we talking about?"

"Nelson. He doesn't know I exist," she blurted, looking flustered. "I heard you and Detective Stevens are not actually going to date now, and well, you did go to the Singles Club. And look at the change in Gary, all because he thought he stood a chance with you. So back to Nelson. I've seen you a few times at his shop lately, and well, I see the way he looks at you. That's all."

"Oh, Milly, I had no idea you liked Nelson. Trust

me, he is only being nice to me because he's a good businessman. Gary is just a friend, in fact, I'm pretty sure Lisa at the bakery has a thing for him. As for Detective Stevens, things are just too complicated right now. If I were going to date anyone, it would be him." I smiled kindly at her. "You should tell Nelson how you feel. I bet he would be interested."

Her pale green eyes widened and filled with hope. "You really think I stand a chance with Nelson?"

"I don't see why not."

"Thank you for everything, Kalli." Appreciation and sincerity shined in her eyes. "I'm sorry if I made you think I didn't like you, or upset you with my insensitive comments. I didn't mean anything by them. I tend to ramble when I'm nervous."

"No worries, Milly. I actually do the same thing." I smiled at her, happy I'd made a new friend. "Speaking of Detective Stevens, I can't help but worry about his ma. Can I ask you a couple questions?"

"Sure. Anything I can do to help."

"Do you know if Nelson had an alibi the night of Ariana's murder?" Her mouth fell open.

"I'm not saying he's the killer," I rushed to add. "I'm just trying to verify he isn't. He said he was home alone in bed at that time, but there's no way to prove it. And he did vow to get even with Ariana as well as Benny for slashing his tires."

Milly was already shaking her head. "I don't know about Ariana's murder, but I do know he was at work during the time Nina Simone was murdered. I walked by at that time and saw him. I would think the killer is the same person who killed both of them, so I highly doubt he's the killer. At least, I sure hope not."

"That makes sense. I'm sure you're right. I'm just trying to cover all possible leads to help clear Chloe's name." We reached the park and were headed over to the fenced in dog section to let them play, when Wolfgang let out a howl and yanked hard.

"Wolfgang Stevens, whoa!" I yelled, but he ignored my command. I'd never run so fast in my life and nearly tipped over Mr. Chew's Ice Cream stand as we came to a jarring stop right in front.

"Well, there's my little buddy." Ji-Hoon Chew filled a doggy cup of vanilla ice cream and raised his eyebrows in question at me.

I nodded yes, still too out of breath to speak.

He came around the front of his stand and set the cup on the ground, then Wolfgang dove in. So much for being a perfect gentleman.

I waved to Milly to let her know I'd catch up with her some other time, then I turned to Ji-Hoon. "What do I owe you for this naughty fellow?"

"It's on the house." He shooed my money away. "Detective Stevens should have warned you Wolfgang is a puller, especially when he sees my stand. Ice cream is his favorite treat in the whole wide world."

"Oh, Detective Stevens warned me, all right, but he could have been a little more specific on what exactly made him pull." I rubbed my shoulder which felt like it had slipped out of its socket. When Wolfgang finished, I pulled out a wipe and was gearing myself up to throw the sticky, gross cup away in a nearby trash can, but Ji-Hoon beat me to it with a sympathetic smile. Thank you so much. I really appreciate it."

Mr. Chew nodded and returned to his popular stand as a line had already formed. I tightened my hand on Wolfgang's leash and turned around to head back over to the dog park when I stopped short. Fender's Food Truck was about thirty feet away, but I would recognize Benny Balboa anywhere.

Benny was eating a hotdog with all the fixings and talking to a large bald-headed man. The same man I'd seen at the community center during the Precious Gems and Jewelry Fair. The same man I'd run into. The same man who had warned me to be careful. New questions ran through my head.

Why was he still in town?

How did he know Benny?

A chill ran down my spine...and why were they both staring at me?

~

A HALF HOUR later after Wolf played with his friends in the dog park, I headed over to Fender's Food Truck. Benny and Baldy were gone, thank goodness. Once again, Wolfgang yanked the leash, but this time I was ready.

"Easy, boy," I said, holding my own until we reached the truck.

Wolfgang apparently didn't mind people or other dogs. He only got excited and out of control when it came to food. I should have known, given the size of him and the fact that his owner was a foodie.

"Hey, Big Boy, you here for your hot dog?" Finneas Fender met my gaze as he held up the hotdog. "Do you mind?"

"Why not? It's obvious his owner doesn't." I laughed.

"Detective Stevens is a regular around here, especially in the summer. And after here, he takes Wolfy to Dino's Doggy Daycare, but their treats aren't nearly as tasty." He winked.

Wolf howled until he cut the hotdog up on a paper plate and set it before him on the ground. Wolf dove in most ungentlemanly like. We'd have to have a talk about that.

"Would you care for anything?" Finneas asked me.

"Oh, no thank you. I'm stuffed." I lied. I was actually starving, but there was no way a food truck could stay clean enough for my peace of mind. I couldn't exactly go around asking people I didn't know that well if I could inspect their kitchens. "I noticed Benny Balboa over here a little while ago. Who was that man with him?"

Finneas shrugged. "Not sure. I think he was in town for the Precious Gems and Jewelry Fair. Most people left town after the murder and getting cleared by the police. Not sure why he stayed, but I did hear them say something about a buyer."

"A buyer for what?"

"I really couldn't say. They walked away before I heard anymore."

"Well, thank you for your help. And for Wolfgang's treat."

"You're very welcome. Tell Detective Stevens I said hi."

"I will."

I walked away with Wolfgang and headed down Main Street back toward my car. We were halfway down the street, when Wolf's fur stiffened, and he let out a low growl. I looked around but didn't see anyone, yet my gut told me I was being watched.

Again.

"Good boy." I pet the top of his head and tightened my hand on the leash. He stopped growling but stayed on high alert. I suddenly saw the value of owning a large dog because if he weren't with me right now, I would be terrified.

Once we reached my Prius, I let Wolf in the backseat with only a slight cringe. I would have to have the inside detailed asap. We drove a couple streets over and arrived at Dino's Doggy Daycare.

After parking the car, I got out with Wolf and headed to the front door. Olivia and Eleanor stepped outside with a wide, surprised smile on their faces.

"I'm doing Detective Stevens a favor by walking Wolfgang and dropping him at daycare," I said.

"We have two full-sized black poodles," Olivia said proudly. "They're sisters from the same litter, just like us."

"And you should see their collars." Eleanor beamed. "Why, they have more bling than we do."

I laughed. "I bet they look fabulous."

"They do indeed." Oliva winked.

Eleanor opened the door for me. "You take care now, dear. These streets aren't safe anymore." She looked around, a breeze kicking up pebbles and dust in the parking lot.

My gaze followed suit, and Wolf let out another low growl.

"Thanks, I will. You, too." I hurried inside with Wolf, absolutely certain of one thing.

I was definitely being followed.

CHAPTER 16

"The yard looks great, Erik," I said as I shut off the engine and stepped out of my car. After dropping Wolf off at daycare, I'd gone into Full Disclosure to do some sketching. I'd just returned home around dinner time.

Jaz pulled in right after me. After the work he'd done on Chloe's yard, Jaz and I had hired him to change up the landscaping in the front of our house. My whole family used my cousin Yanni for their yards, but we'd specifically requested Erik. It looks like that had turned out to be a smart decision.

"Wow, that looks fantastic," Jaz agreed. "I love all the flowering bushes and colored stones. It's so pretty."

He nodded in acknowledgement, a man of few words I was finding out. Running a hand over his beard then fixing his short ponytail, he looked uncomfortable with praise. "Thanks. Glad you both like it."

"Detective Stevens' back yard is a mess. Maybe you can mow for him and put it on my bill," I said.

"Already took care of it." Erik pulled his hat down lower over his face to shield it from the sun. "It's the least I could do for his mother's recommendation. I'm getting requests all over town."

"That's great. I'm sure he'll appreciate it." I smiled.

He nodded again. "Enjoy the rest of your day, Ladies." He gathered the rest of his things and stowed them in the trailer attached to the Yanni's Yards company truck then drove off.

Moments later Nik pulled in the driveway with his old partner, Darnell. They got out of the car and joined us.

"Nice landscaping," Nik said, looking around the yard and eyeing the new walkway. "Your cousin do that?"

"Actually, that new guy Erik did," I said. "He mowed your yard by the way. Said he owed you one."

"That was nice of him." Nik shrugged, shoving his hands in his sport coat pockets. "I was going to get to it this weekend."

"Right," Jaz chimed in. "Even I'm not buying that one." She smiled wide at Darnell, who actually blushed. "I see you brought your friend home for dinner."

"I kind of invited myself," Darnell finally said after shaking off Jaz's spell. "What can I say. I can't resist his mother's cooking."

"Care to join us after for a drink?" I offered, locking eyes with Nik. "Maybe we can catch up and share notes."

"It's a date." His lips twitched. Nikos was back, pushing the limits as usual.

I rolled my eyes. "See you in an hour for a *drink* and sharing notes, that's all."

I followed Jaz into our half of the house and set my things down while she headed into her bedroom to change. I looked around for my cat but couldn't find her. That was strange. I happen to glance outside. Ms. Priss was out on the deck with the sliding door closed. I slid the door open and let her in. "How did you get out there, you little Houdini?"

I always let her out when I was home, but I left the door open a little so she could get back in. I would never go to work and leave her outside with the door closed. I fed her as Jaz came back into the kitchen.

"Wow, she's thirsty," Jaz said. "Look at her drink all that water. That's not usually like her. Maybe you should change the brand of food you're using. Maybe it has too much sodium or something."

"It's not the food or too much sodium. It's because she's been out in the heat all day long." I frowned.

Jaz's eyes sprang wide. "Seriously? You left her outside all day? That's not like you, either."

"You know I triple check everything. I did not leave the door open this morning. Did you?" I asked.

"No way. I know what a freak you are about that kind of stuff, especially with a killer still on the loose around town."

"Then how did she get out?" I didn't wait for an answer as I looked all around the house. I quickly changed my clothes before coming back into the kitchen. "Jaz, you left the bathroom window open. The screen was pushed out."

She bit her bottom lip, heating up the takeout she'd brought home for dinner. "Sorry. I thought I closed it. I'll be more careful from now on."

I opened a bottle of wine. "It's okay. I'm just a little spooked after seeing Benny with that guy I told you about from the Precious Gems and Jewelry Fair." I took a sip of wine. "And I keep feeling like someone is watching me. Wolfgang acted so strange a couple times today, and I'm pretty sure I was followed in broad daylight."

Jaz brought the takeout to the kitchen table, and we both sat down and took a moment to dig into our dinners. I had made a salad, not trusting the takeout. "I'm going to gain a ton of weight if Boomer doesn't quit feeding me."

"Oh, please, you look fabulous. You love the attention. Speaking of which, ease up on poor Detective Johnson. I don't think the man can handle all of you."

"I'm not doing a thing. I can't help it if men get tongue tied around me," she said. "You know my heart belongs to my hunky detective."

A knock sounded on our door.

"Speaking of hunky detectives." Jaz jumped up and opened the door without even looking.

I sighed, shaking my head.

"Come in, gentlemen." She smiled wide.

Nik and Darnell walked through the door, and Jaz started to close it.

"Not so fast, darlin'," Boomer said, then kissed her on the mouth, making her jump in surprise. He was the only man I knew who could surprise Jaz. That was why I was pretty sure they were going to last. "Did you save any dinner for me?"

"Always." She hugged him then joined us in the kitchen.

We all sat around the table. Jaz got them all a beer and poured herself a glass of wine. I filled them in on what had happened so far.

"What do you think it means?" I asked.

"I did some checking like Nik asked me to," Darnell said, earning narrowed eyes from Boomer toward Nik, but Boomer kept quiet.

Jaz had said if it had been Boomer's mother, he

would be doing the same thing. He just didn't want to know about it so he wouldn't have to outright lie to the captain if he asked him for details. Boomer was always around. It was inevitable he would be around conversation regarding the case.

Darnell looked between the two detectives, and then asked Nik, "Should I continue, partner?"

Nik raised a brow at Boomer, who sighed and nodded. "Go ahead, Darnell. The more ears we have on this, the better."

Darnell continued. "My informants back in the city tell me Benny's definitely been working with some underground black-market rings. He's collecting jewelry like Ariana's and Nina Simone's late husband's things, then turning around and pawning them off as genuine pieces for much more than they're worth, making a huge profit."

"Do we know who his buyers are?" Nik asked.

"We don't know who the buyers are, but you can probably guess who is setting up the deals."

"Who?" Boomer asked, intrigued.

"The Tedesco Family." Darnell gave Nik a meaningful look.

"Wait. Isn't that the mob family Benny was linked to when he dated Ariana?" Boomer asked, running a hand through his russet curls.

"One and the same," Nik said, clenching his jaw. "That's not a family you want to mess with."

"It gets better," Darnell added, then looked at me. "The bald man you saw Benny with sounds exactly like Antonio Tedesco himself. I hate to say it, but if he's interested in you, that's not a good thing."

And just like that I lost my appetite.

SUNDAY BRUNCH WAS at my family's house since Chloe still wasn't allowed back at her place. Not to mention, Nik didn't want her to be alone now that he knew Tedesco was hanging around town. He didn't want me alone either after hearing about my hunch that someone was following me, and that I'd run into Tedesco a couple times already.

"You need to move in with your mama so I can take care of you." Ma fussed over me, bringing me more food and trying to feed me as if I were still five. "You no eat enough. You're skin and bones."

"I'm not moving home, Ma." I stepped away from her hovering hands. "And I'm not too thin."

"Bones break down with just skin on them," Aunt Tasoula said. "I know these things. Cousin Esmerelda had the crack in the bones, the ostyperogies, because she no eat enough. She had no muscle, just skin and bones and rubber bands holding her body together. Her mama fed her too much Jell-O. It's true."

"I'm pretty sure her skin and rubber bands and Jell-O aren't what caused the *osteoporosis*. It was a lack of calcium, not the amount of food she ate," I responded. "Doc LaLone says my bones are just fine."

"The perogies aren't going to break your bones," Pop said, manning the grill beneath the gazebo in our back yard. "The mob will if they catch up with you. Mark my words. I don't like that big bald man looking at my daughter."

"Big bald man, with the scary big hands, run as fast as you can, singing catch me if you can," Frona sang as she skipped around the gazebo as if she was on a merry go round, over and over and over.

"Frona, stop. You're making me dizzy." YiaYia fanned her face while she sat in a chair off to the side.

"Come help me fix a plate," Papou said, distracting her.

My life might be a circus in this back yard, but I knew what I was getting. I was genuinely afraid of the unknown world outside this safe haven.

"It's no crime for him to be in town." Nik stepped over to my side. "Unfortunately, we have to wait until he does something illegal to make a move. Just be aware of your surroundings, and stay alert." His gaze held mine. "And stop going rogue. I'm too young to have gray hairs sprouting."

"Okay."

"Okay? Just like that? What's the catch?"

"No catch. I'm actually nervous being alone, and I don't like that feeling." I folded my arms over my chest.

"You're not alone, bestie." Jaz gave me a hug. "You always have me."

"Like you would be any better than Kalli at fending off a mobster." Boomer's expression looked strained. "I don't want either one of you alone anywhere. I'm teaching you both self-defense."

"That's not a bad idea," Nik agreed. "At least then you stand a fighting chance of saving yourself if you do get attacked."

"Oh, I want to learn," Thalia and Eleni both said.

"So do we," Ma said, more to herself and Aunt Tasoula.

"Nikos already taught me years ago." Chloe beamed proudly.

"You're never too old to learn how to defend yourselves," Darnell said. "The three of us could divide the rest of you all up in groups and finish in half the time."

"I'm sure Shelly Tarzia will let us use a room in her gym, The Twilight Zone Athletic Club. It's open twenty-four hours a day. She used to be a cop," Boomer added.

"Done." Nik nodded.

The women of all generations squealed excitedly, talking at once, giving me a raging headache. What had we gotten ourselves into?

Just then, Nelson Rockwell came running into my parents' backyard, out of breath and looking pale.

"Where is she?" he gasped.

"Who?" my father asked.

"Ms. Stevens. Chloe. I must find her at once. I tried calling, but she didn't answer her phone."

Chloe stepped forward. "Well, Mr. Rockwell, calm yourself down. You're going to have a heart attack. I'm right here. I'm sorry, I didn't hear my phone with all the excitement going on around here. What did you want to tell me?"

"It's gone," he said and looked ready to cry.

"What's gone?" Nik asked, his face looking grave.

"The heirloom necklace. I doubled my security, but it didn't matter. The Bandit struck again. This time, it was the only item taken from my shop. I'm so sorry, Ms. Stevens, but it looks like the Pagonis family heirloom necklace has been stolen."

CHAPTER 17

My ma sent me to Sal's Supermarket with a mile long list of groceries. We'd just finished Sunday brunch, yet she was already planning a five-course meal to take Chloe's mind off her troubles. The poor woman was distraught over the family heirloom necklace getting stolen from Rockwell Jewelers. She blamed herself for having it appraised. She never planned on selling it, so what was the point in knowing how much it was worth? The only thing that did was put them all in danger and the necklace in jeopardy of greedy people.

Now it was gone, never to be handed down to her grandchildren.

Detective Stevens and Detective Matheson were both working together on the case, and Detective Johnson was helping as well. The first person they planned to question was Benny Balboa. If anyone knew anything about missing jewelry, it would be him.

"Hi, Sal," I said, stepping up to the office window.

Salvatore Stallone had bought the old grocery store ten years ago, renovating it into Sal's Supermarket, which had quickly become a town favorite. Each section was skillfully arranged and neatly stocked, the floors sparkling clean, with pleasant music filtering through the sound system. Good lighting and wide aisles made shopping a breeze, and the shopping carts were sanitized regularly. The deli might not be as good as my cousins Kosmos and Silas Diner Delights, but his produce was second to none.

"Hey, Kalli," Sal responded with a grave look on his smooth round cheeks. "I heard what happened to the Pagonis family heirloom necklace. That's such a shame." He shook his thick head of dark hair. "Clearview used to be a place I was proud to raise my kids in, but I'm afraid to let them loose these days."

"I don't know what's going on around here with all these burglaries and people dying. This is turning out to be one scary summer."

"Hang on a minute?" He pushed away from his computer and stepped down out of the office to stand next to me in his dockers, dress shirt, and tie. "There, that's better. Sitting up high in that office is fine when I'm working, but I don't like talking through that window. It's so impersonal. Now, then, is there anything I can do to help?"

I handed him my ma's list. "Ma sent me to get all of these things. Honestly, I don't even know what half of these items are or where to look for them. Let's just say I don't take after my parents in the cooking department."

"No problem. I'll get these for you, and you can browse around for anything else you might like."

"Thanks, Sal."

He grabbed a shopping cart and my list, then headed toward the produce and meat departments. Meanwhile, I started roaming the aisles, looking for anything I thought Chloe might like. I normally only shopped in the health food section, but I figured today might call for a little comfort food.

I was reading the label on a box of snack mix, shuddering over words I couldn't pronounce and the thought of what they could do to my insides, when I heard voices one aisle over. Curious, I rounded the corner and stopped short.

"Oh, hi, you two," I said, feeling as awkward as Rex at the moment. I smoothed my sundress, still wearing the clothes I'd worn to church and brunch, yet squirming as if I'd been caught sinning.

Gary and Lisa jumped apart, looking red-faced and guilty.

"We were just—"

"This isn't what—"

They spoke at once.

I held up a hand. "Honestly, it's none of my business what you two do together, really. I'm happy for you both." I was thrilled to see his interests had turned elsewhere. Lisa was a pretty brunette and more his age. They actually made a cute couple.

"You are?" Lisa asked, looking doubtful.

"Yes," I reassured her. "Gary and I are just friends, right, Gary?"

"Absolutely," Gary said. "Lisa and I really clicked, and it just kind of happened. You and I didn't have the same spark. Besides, I knew you still had a thing for Detective Stevens, even if you refuse to admit it."

"I'm not in a position to date anyone right now," I said, neither confirming nor denying my feelings for Nik, though my pink cheeks were probably giving me away.

Sal came around the corner with a full cart. "There you are, Kalli." He nodded to Gary and Lisa. "And here are all the things on your mother's list."

"You're a life saver, Sal." I took the cart from him.

"No problem. My daughter will ring you up at the front. Give your family my best, and Detective Steven's family, too."

"I will," I said, then waved goodbye to Gary and Lisa.

Ten minutes later, I headed out back to the parking lot to load my car with my grocery bags. Wilma's Wine and Spirits was right next door. I locked my car and walked around to the front to enter the liquor store.

Wilma Merryweather stood behind the counter, somehow pulling off her snow-white hair buzzed close to her head. The woman put the fabulous in fifty, looking stunning with her intricate tattoos, nose ring and ear piercings. I envied her confidence, which was something I lacked but was working hard on correcting. I was hoping the self-defense class we were supposed to take later this week would help.

I walked up behind a tall, willowy woman who was checking out. When the woman turned around, I blinked in surprise. "Thalia, what are you doing here?" Not that she didn't have a right to be there, I was just surprised to run into her at that moment.

She held up a bottle of Ouzo and chardonnay.

"Ma?"

"How'd you guess." She laughed.

"That's what I was coming in for, but seeing as how you just bought them, I'll get the groceries over to the restaurant before they spoil. You know how Ma gets if anything is left out of the fridge for more than a minute."

"My ma is the same way. Aunt Chloe, too. We waste more food because it touched the air for too long." She shook her chic bobbed hairdo, which really did suit her face better than the long hair had, and laughed. Everyone except me had ended up with the perfect hairstyle, yet mine was *still* deflating.

"Thanks for your help, Thalia. I appreciate it, and so does Ma." She squeezed my shoulder, and I suddenly had the strongest sense that Thalia was in danger. "Hey, be careful, okay?"

"Of course. I always am." She looked at me a little funny. "And you're welcome. I'm sure I'll see you at your parents' restaurant later when they insist on feeding us again." She carried her box of alcohol and left the store with a nod as she headed to her car parked out front on the street.

I followed her out and started to walk back to my car in the grocery store parking lot when I realized I'd dropped my keys in the liquor store. Turning around with a sigh, I went back for them. Ma was going to have a spell if I was late. I saw Thalia pull away from the curb as I went into the store. Spotting my car keys on the floor, I bent down to pick them up. When I stood back up, a movement caught my eye.

Through the window, I saw Baldy pull away from the curb in a black car. Baldy as in Antonio Tedesco, Scary Mob Guy. Running outside before he disappeared completely, I watched where he went. Way down the street was Nik's cousin's car with Baldy not far behind.

If I wasn't mistaken, he was following Thalia.

I ran back to the parking lot, jumped in my Prius, and pulled around front as quickly as I could. By the time I drove onto the street, they were gone.

∼

"Baldy's after Thalia," I blurted into my phone as I raced down the road to my parents' restaurant.

"What are you talking about?" Nik asked through the other end of the line.

"I saw him follow her after she left the liquor store."

"Who is Baldy?"

"Sorry, Antonio Tedesco."

A pause filled the line. "Are you sure?"

"Positive."

"I'll let Detective Matheson and Detective Johnson know. We'll split up and see what we can find. Hang on." He made a call I could hear in the background. "Okay, they're on it. We just got done talking to Benny Balboa, who claims he doesn't know anything about the theft of the necklace. Said he was at the Clearview Motel, sleeping off the night before at Flannigan's Pub. I checked with Michael Flannigan and with Larry Miller. His story checks out." Nik let out a sigh, and I could hear the exhaustion in his voice.

"That doesn't mean Baldy, I mean Tedesco, couldn't have stolen it. We know they're working together on pawning the fakes. Who's to say they wouldn't gladly welcome the real deal."

"I don't trust either of them," Nik agreed. "I know Thalia said she met with Benny in secret to warn him off, but you don't have lunch with someone you're warning off. I just hope that whatever she's hiding is something she can handle on her own because she's clearly not talking to me or asking for my help."

"I agree," I said. I believed she really didn't like Benny and wanted him to stay away from her friends and family because I'd heard her thoughts, but there was more to her story, and I still didn't know what *I have to finish this* meant.

"Gotta go. I think I see his car." Nik hung up.

The line went dead, and my overactive imagination started spinning out of control. My heart started racing as I drove to Aphrodite's to drop off the groceries for my ma. What if Baldy had Thalia in the trunk of his car? What if he was going to finish her off before she could finish whatever *this* was? Wasn't that what the mob did? Take people out? Off them? Was I next?

I could feel my blood pump furiously through my veins. What if the blood was coursing through my veins too fast, and my veins burst before I could stop the car? All of Ma's groceries would spoil, and Chloe would never get her comfort meal. Who would comfort Ma when I was gone? My chest felt heavy, like an elephant was sitting on it. Stars swam before my eyes as I pulled into the parking lot of my parents' restaurant.

Was I having a heart attack?

I reached into the glove box and pulled out the emergency paper bag I kept in there. Putting it to my mouth, I closed my eyes as I slowly breathed in and out over and over until I could feel my pulse return to normal. I knew what this was, I thought, as my reasoning returned. I hadn't had a full-blown panic attack in ages.

A knock on my window made me jump out of my skin.

I rolled it down. "Hi, Ma."

"Kalli, what's wrong? Why are you late? What happened? You look pale." She felt my forehead. *And my groceries are spoiling in this heat. What did I do to deserve drama drama drama with this one?*

I brushed her hand aside. "It's Thalia," I finally said. "She's in trouble. Baldy. Bad guy. Chased her."

"Bow to your partner, bow to your foe, let's chase Baldy, here we go." Frona skipped around my car, making me dizzy.

"Thalia's not in trouble, Kalli." She eyed me as I climbed out of my car. I fanned my face, needing air. She waved for her employees to unload the groceries. "I'm calling Doc LaLone again. I think your cussed brain has gotten worse."

"It's not my head, Ma." I followed her inside the restaurant's back door to the kitchen. "I'm telling you; I went to the grocery store like you asked me to. Sal was so nice to get all the things you had on your list, by the way." I tended to ramble when I was frazzled, and today I'd had was enough to frazzle even the calmest person. "Then I went to the liquor store to get the alcohol, but Thalia was there and had already gotten it."

"Because I asked her to. If I'd wanted you to get the alcohol, I would have added it to your list. When are you going to listen to your mama?"

"I know, I know, Ma. So, I left, but realized I'd dropped my keys. So, I went back to get my keys, and I saw Baldy follow her."

"Baldy? Who's Baldy?"

"Ugh, the mob guy. Antonio Tedesco of the Tedesco Family. I called Detective Stevens, and he saw Baldy's car while we were on the phone, which sent me into a panic all over again. I nearly had a heart attack imaging what was going on, then I realized it was just a panic attack, and well, now I'm here with semi-spoiled groceries."

"Ah, well why didn't you say so. That makes more sense. Many men are bald. I mean, you really need to start using your words, Kalliope. Baldy could be anyone." She shook her head. "You're fine. Let's eat."

"Ma, are you hearing what I'm saying?"

"Hearing, yes." Her forehead wrinkled. "Understanding you, not so much. And now you give me the frown lines. I should tox the bow like your Aunt Tasoula is always trying to get me to do."

"I repeat. Thalia is in trouble."

"I am?" Thalia asked from the doorway, and that was all it took.

I burst into tears and sat on the floor.

Frona sang Duck Duck Goose and skipped to the lou around me.

Thalia called Nik.

And Ma called Doc LaLone.

CHAPTER 18

"What are you doing here, Ballas?" Detective Stevens asked me all businesslike as I joined him at the Clearview Motel the next day.

"Visiting my friend, Gary," I lied.

Doc had declared I didn't have a nervous breakdown, after all. I'd just had an *episode*, he'd called it, which he'd said was understandable given all the stress I'd been under lately. Thank you very much, at least someone understood what it was like to be me, unlike the stubborn detective beside me. Not to mention my family, but that was a whole other story. Still, Doc had suggested that it would be a good idea if I took a few days off from work and got some rest.

Who could rest at a time like this?

I know what I saw. That car had definitely belonged to Baldy. I was positive he was tailing Thalia, but Nik said my lead led to a dead end. Jaz wouldn't let me in her shop, doctor's orders, and my family wouldn't let me near their restaurant. Then there was Detective Dreamy who would lock me up if given the chance. My family and friends all claimed it was for my own good, but I was more inclined to believe they didn't want my *episodes* scaring their customers away.

The only way I would rest was if my life returned to normal. That meant solving these murders and catching a bandit. So, when I'd heard Penelope Drakos had discovered her hotel room was broken into this morning after she'd returned from breakfast, I'd found an excuse to stop by.

"Yeah, I'm not buying that for a minute, Ballas," Nik responded, eyeing me suspiciously. "You need to—"

"Gary, oh my goodness. I can't believe the news." I stepped around Detective Dreamy and rushed over to the counter. "Don't worry, it wasn't your fault. You're doing such a good job around here. Everyone says so."

"Thanks." He swiped a hand through is sandy blond waves then loosened the collar of his polo shirt. "Larry isn't too happy with me."

"Why?"

"I was on duty this morning and supposed to be watching the monitors, but it's a Monday morning. Things are slow around here during that time, so I figured it would be okay." He ran his hand over his jaw in need of shaving.

"Okay for what?" Nik asked, joining me as he studied the man, probably thinking the same thing I was. Gary looked a little less put together this morning.

"To have a friend over," Gary admitted, looking around and then leaning forward as he lowered his voice. "Part of the perks of working here is I get room and board for free. I'm finally out of my mother's place."

"Good for you on getting your act together," Nik said, sounding sincere. "I'm sure your mother is proud, but rules are rules. You probably should have had your friend over on your own time and not when you were supposed to be working."

"I agree, and I apologized to Larry. It's just new and exciting. I made a mistake. I just hope Larry won't fire me. I told him it won't happen again. He's with Mrs. Drakos down the hall in room fifteen."

I patted Gary's hand. "It will be okay, Gary."

"I sure hope so." He closed his eyes for a minute. *I can't lose Lisa, not after everything's she's been through.*

"Where is your friend now?" I asked gently.

He blew out a breath. "At work I think." *She couldn't risk staying here any longer, that's for sure.*

I let go of his hand, not wanting to intrude any more than I had to. "I'll see you later, Gary. Hang in there." What had Lisa been through and why couldn't she risk being here any longer? I wondered as I made my way down the hall until I reached Penelope's room. Nik was already inside, talking to her. I stood just outside the door, peeking through the crack and listening.

"They went through Ariana's things," Penelope said on a sniffle. "It's all I have left of her. Why would someone go through her things?"

"That's what we're here to find out, Mrs. Drakos." Nik looked around the room, writing notes in a notebook. "Was anything taken?"

"Not that I can tell." She shook her head, looking around the room in dismay. "The place is a mess, as if someone was in a hurry and just threw everything all over the place searching for something."

"Do you think it could have been the Business Bandit, Detective Stevens?" Larry adjusted his glasses. "I really didn't think he would hit up my motel. I mean, even I can admit it's not that fancy. I can't imagine what he would want from here."

"That's why I don't think it was him. The Bandit is a pro. He never messes things up because there's more risk of leaving behind clues that way. Not to mention, he doesn't hit places and take nothing. He's strategic about his targets." Nik tapped his pen on his notebook. "Whoever did this was an amateur."

"Well, if it's not the work of the Bandit, then I have no clue who it could be." Penelope's eyes widened. "Unless it was the killer. Oh my Zeus, do you think they came back here to kill me, too?"

"I don't think so, Mrs. Drakos. If the killer wanted you dead, they've had plenty of chances to take a shot at you by now." Nik flipped through his notes. "Maybe if it was the killer, they were looking for something they thought Ariana still had. Did she ever say anything about what was going on with her? Why she came here to begin with?"

"I don't know. I'm so sorry about that, Nikos. I really am. I was just as surprised as anyone that she was never pregnant to begin with." Her tears started to flow. "I feel like I didn't even know my own daughter."

I couldn't help myself; I came into the room.

Nik's head snapped up, and he frowned at me, but I ignored him.

I hugged Penelope, and she hugged me back hard and wouldn't let go. I tried not to squirm because I sensed she needed this. "It's okay, Penelope. You *did* know her. Sometimes the people we're closest to do things we never imagined possible, and sometimes they have no choice. We all have our secrets."

"You have no idea," she said. *And sometimes those secrets make us want to kill them for it.*

I let go of her, a bit startled, then I stepped back.

Nik gave me an odd look.

I wiped my hands on my shorts as discreetly as I could, and Nik got the message. Let him think it was my quirks. I needed time to figure out how to explain to him what I'd just heard.

"Larry, do you keep a security camera?" Detective Steven's asked, back in investigative mode.

Larry nodded.

"The Bandit wouldn't have been careless enough to slip up, but this amateur might have been. Can we take a look at this morning's video?"

"Sure thing. Follow me."

We all made our way back to the lobby. Gary stood behind the front desk, not quite meeting Larry's eyes. Larry might be forgiving, but Penelope gave him an evil look as we walked by. A few minutes later, we were in the office, and Larry had this morning's video pulled up.

Sure enough, a person with a nondescript black hooded sweatshirt walked into the screen, smart enough not to park their car in the parking lot. The person slipped through the front door and made their way past an empty lobby, then down the hall to room fifteen. The person was tall and too big, but that's about all you could see. They wore gloves and opened the door, but it was impossible to tell anything else about them. They trashed the place. A noise sounded down the hall, and the person quickly left, returning past the lobby and out the door with no one the wiser.

"Whoever did this got ahold of a key somehow," Nik pointed out. "It's possible they knew Penelope."

"Or they're the killer and took Ariana's key when they killed her," I added, earning a contemplative look from the detective.

"At least this video is something to go on," Detective Stevens said, making more notes. "It's a start."

"Wait, Larry," Penelope said. "Don't turn that off."

The video kept rolling. Gary appeared on the screen as he walked down the hall, returning to the front desk, with a woman by his side. He stopped, turned her to face him, and kissed her goodbye.

"Pause that," Penelope blurted, and Larry complied. Penelope tensed. "Who is that woman?"

"I'm guessing Gary's friend," Larry said. "Don't worry. I told him he's not allowed to fraternize while on duty anymore."

"I don't care what he does." Her eyes were locked on that screen. "I just want to know who that woman is. She looks familiar. Can you zoom in closer?"

Larry squinted at the screen and played with the tape, finally was able to zoom in on the woman's face.

Penelope let out a shriek.

Nik reached for his gun.

I slapped a hand over my mouth.

"What in tarnation is all the screaming about, woman? That's just Lisa Chamberlain." Larry pushed his glasses back up his nose. "She's the bookkeeper for Maria's bakery, Sinfully Delicious. I heard she's pretty good."

"She's not good. She's bad," Penelope spat, looking crazed as she stared at the screen with pure evil in her eyes. "She's the woman who had an affair with my husband."

~

Penelope had stormed off, not listening to any of us, as she headed straight for Sinfully Delicious. Nik and I and even Gary, once he got wind of what was going on, took off after her. Lucky for Gary, Larry actually liked him. He told him he would man the front desk, and for him to go get this mess sorted out.

Stepping into the bakery was like stepping into the audience of an off-Broadway drama...or attending a Sunday brunch with my family.

"How dare you follow me to Clearview," Penelope accused Lisa, thrusting her finger in the woman's direction.

"Calm down, Mrs. Drakos. I know you've suffered a great loss, but stirring up drama is what got you and your daughter in this mess in the first place," Maria said with a calm but firm voice, somehow looking taller than she was. "You can't come into my business and just do what you want." Lisa hid behind Maria, who might be petite, but was a force to be reckoned with when it came to her employees.

"This woman isn't who she says she is." Penelope stabbed a finger at Lisa. "She used to work for my husband."

"Is that true?" Maria asked Lisa, a wary look transforming her face. "I won't condone lying."

Tears were streaming down Lisa's face. "Yes, it's true, but I never lied to you. I told you I worked at a restaurant. I just didn't mention that Castor was Penelope's deceased husband because I knew she would try to ruin me from starting over any place I went. I didn't follow her, I promise. I was here first. I had no idea she and her daughter would come to Clearview. You have to believe me."

"None of this is Lisa's fault," Gary said, walking behind the counter and taking Lisa in his arms.

"What do you know?" Penelope raged, turning her hatred onto him. "You're just a no-good drunk."

"You can't talk to him like that," Lisa said, finding

the courage to straighten her spine. "He didn't do anything wrong."

"It's okay," Gary said to her. "She's right. I was a drunk. She copes with her loss with anger. I coped with mine by trying to drink myself to death. I'm a changed man now, and that's because of you."

"Why would you want anyone who sleeps with a married man? She only distracted you so she could have her accomplice break into my room. I'm sure she stole the key from you without you even knowing. She's manipulative like that. She's not going to get away with it this time."

"Careful making unsubstantiated accusations, Mrs. Drakos," Nik warned gently. "You were wrong before, remember?"

Penelope threw her hands up in the air, but hesitated for a moment. "Well, what am I supposed to think?"

"I didn't know Castor was married when I first went to work for him," Lisa said, taking advantage of the pause. "You were never in the restaurant back then. When I found out, I tried to break things off. He kept saying you had cheated on him first and your marriage had been over with for years. That he was going to leave you. I was never with him again after I found out about you, but I needed the work. I couldn't quit. My mother was sick, and I was the only one who could help pay for her medical treatment. Then after Castor died, you found out and fired me. My mother died that same year."

Penelope looked at Lisa, studying her as if in a new light. "Castor was not a good man," she finally conceded. "I want justice, Detective Stevens. I want to know who the person was in that video. Someone has to pay."

"And they will," Nik said. "I promise you. But you have to stop losing control, and let me do my job."

"Okay," she agreed. "But I want to know the minute you find out anything."

"You've got a deal," Nik said, but I knew him well enough to know his body language. He'd seen something he didn't like in that video, and I wanted to know what it was.

CHAPTER 19

The next morning, I stood beside a thick mat, feeling overwhelmed and nervous and a little creeped out. I swear I could smell sweat permeating the room, making a beeline for my pores. I kept willing them to close tight, but somehow didn't think that was possible. I'd have to take a hot shower and steam them clean later. My eyes kept staring at the mat wondering just how thoroughly it had been cleaned, and I curled my bare toes in response.

I might never recover from this.

Ma, Aunt Tasoula, Eleni, Thalia, Jaz and I were in a private room in the Twilight Zone Athletic Club, full of mats and mirrors. Since Nik had already taught his ma self-defense moves years ago, she'd stayed home.

Shelly Tarzia, a former police officer, was a petite thing but intimidating and full of muscles. She was as tough as all three detectives, and she loved to let them know it. She had gone over a bunch of safety tips about how to be aware of your surroundings. And then she had told us there were about eighty moves when it came to defending oneself, but she'd chosen six moves she thought would be most effective for women like us. So, we'd spent the last half hour practicing them, but it was hard to keep them all straight. I was terrified my mind would go blank the second someone confronted me.

"Okay, ladies, let's see what you've got," Shelly said.

She wanted to *test* us? I tried to swallow, but my throat was dry. I'd never been good at taking tests.

"A test? I no like tests," Ma said, crossing her arms stubbornly. "My husband tests my patience every day."

"It's true," Aunt Tasoula added. "He's lucky to still be alive with this one. Trust me, I know. I grew up with her."

"I think she means test our moves on a fake attacker," Eleni chimed in, looking excited as she eyed the detectives.

"Exactly," Shelly confirmed. "Let's take Detective Stevens for instance." Shelly motioned him onto the mat and positioned him in the middle, turning him so he was faced...oh, good lord, *me*! She motioned me forward, and I reluctantly complied, my stomach full of knots. "He's a big strong guy," Shelly said, giving his large bicep a squeeze, "but if you know what to do, you *can* fend him off." She gave him a jab to his ribs and he grunted, then chuckled and rubbed his side.

"If you say so." I looked up the impressive length of him doubtfully. I felt comfortable around Nik, but I'd never had to fight him.

He peeled off his hoodie and tossed it aside, making even my ma gasp. My throat was so dry suddenly. He had on faded gray sweatpants and a sapphire blue tank top, making the brilliant blue of his eyes pop. His olive skin was even more tan from the summer sun, and his muscles looked even bigger than

I remembered, making his intimidation factor skyrocket.

I unzipped my warm-up jacket and tossed it to the edge of the mat with the detective's sweatshirt, my skin much paler than his. I was an *adopted* Greek. It was safe to say my pale skin had never tanned. His eyes flickered and his gaze dropped lower, then quickly snapped back up to my face. My cheeks flushed pink. I didn't have to read his mind to know his thoughts at this moment.

My V-neck T-shirt was the same peach as the stripe on my warm-up pants, as well as the peach on my nails and toes, thanks to Jaz's insistence. Not having worn the outfit in a very long time, it was a bit snugger than I remembered. I tugged at the hem discreetly to no avail and then curled my bare toes self-consciously. Shelly had suggested we take our socks off so we wouldn't slip on the mat, but that only made me feel naked and vulnerable and well, grossed out.

I bit my bottom lip, and Nik's blue gaze softened.

"Remember, it's just me," he said gently, the familiar tone of his voice resonating deep inside and calming me. "I'm not going to hurt you, but I don't want you to worry about hurting me. I want you to think of me as a real attacker and do everything you can to fight me off. Besides, I'm wearing rib pads and a cup." He knocked on his cup twice, and I could feel the blood rush to my face and my ears burn hot.

"Who's there?" Aunt Tasoula said, looking around.

"Nobody you want to come in, you nitwit." Ma rolled her eyes.

"Then what was the knock knock for?"

"To be sure nothing comes out. He's, uh, protecting the parts."

"The parts?" Aunt Tasoula's eyes scrunched up,

dropped lower, and then finally widened. "Oh, the parts. Good boy, Nikos." She knocked twice on her head. "Your mama will want the grandbabies."

Shoot. Me. Now.

"Okay, Kalli." Shelly smiled reassuringly and patted my back. "You've got this. I want you to focus. Soften him up whatever way you can, and then do the moves to escape. If you forget something, remember that it's better to do something than to do nothing. *Always* fight back. Ready?"

I nodded, feeling anything but ready.

Patty called out in a loud voice, "The Wedge!"

One minute Nik was standing before me, just staring at me intensely. That was scary enough, but then he reached out lightning quick and wrapped his huge hands around my throat in a choking move. *Come on, baby, you've got this. It's all muscle memory.* Panic seized me, even though his thoughts and logic told me he wouldn't hurt me, but that didn't stop my adrenaline from soaring. With my heartbeat hammering in my chest, I quickly assessed my situation.

He was too tall for me to reach up and chop my hands down at his elbows. Instead, I clasped my hands together, making sure my fingers were not intertwined so it would be easier to get out of the hold if he grabbed them. Straightening my arms, I formed a wedge shape and swung up as hard as I could, which broke his hold on my neck. Then I swung my clasped hands back down, grazing the front of his nose. I quickly pulled them in and punched forward as hard as I could until I hit him square in the chest. Surprised, he stumbled back a couple of steps, his thoughts revealed by the shock written all over his face, followed quickly by pride.

I blinked, my lips parting slightly. Did I really just do that?

"That's my girl," Jaz shouted.

"Next up," Shelly yelled.

I moved off the mat, and Thalia jumped quickly into my place. Eleni pouted with disappointment.

Shelly didn't give her time to protest. Instead, she called out the next attack. "Hammering Buck!"

I realized that in reality, if Nik were a real attacker, he wouldn't just stop after one move. He would keep coming at his prey until he got what he wanted. Thalia braced herself. Nik rushed forward and wrestled her to the ground. Not a hard task given his six-foot-plus muscled frame. She might be tall, but she was slim. Next, he climbed on top of her, straddling her hips. Once again, he wrapped those big deadly hands of his around her throat. I felt even more vulnerable for her because she was on the ground, with such a large attacker on top of her.

Flashbacks of the night of my concussion hit me square in the gut, robbing me of coherent thought and air. Everything I'd felt that night came rushing back to crush me: the exploding pain in my head and the feelings of fear and helplessness after Erik had saved me. If he hadn't been there, I might have died. Nik was right. I needed this class more than ever. I thought I might faint. My mouth grew dry, and twinkling stars began to dance before my eyes, but then I locked gazes with Nik's sympathetic one.

Suddenly, I knew everything would be okay.

Nik's distraction was all Thalia needed to gain the advantage.

Shelly hollered, "Soften him up."

Thalia balled her hands into fists and jabbed them into Nik's sides as hard as she could. Nik grunted. That seemed to spur her on even more. She hooked her heels over the top of his feet and then poked him hard in the armpit with her straight, stiffened fingers. He flinched, and she didn't hesitate. She grabbed his elbow with her other hand and lifted her hips off the floor, bucking hard and to the side as she pushed him off of her and scrambled to her feet.

"Yeah!" she shouted, fist pumping the air while smiling and painting.

"Eleni, cover the Flame!" Shelly yelled.

Eleni shoved Thalia out of the way and scrambled onto the mat. Nik rolled to his feet as well and from out of nowhere Detective Matheson took his place, a gun appearing in his hands. It was fake, but it looked real enough to all our untrained eyes apparently.

"Fibrillate me." Ma clutched her heart.

"Stop, drop, roll." Aunt Tasoula hit the floor.

Boomer didn't miss a beat as he pointed the gun directly at Eleni's head. She looked like she didn't even have to think about it. She simply reacted on instinct, and the moves came to her. She dropped down below the gun with feet spread wide apart and knees bent in a sumo stance as she grabbed his wrist with one hand and the barrel of the gun with the other, pushing up hard all in one motion.

Then she yanked his bent wrist down until it couldn't bend back any further and wrenched the gun out of his hands, tossing it to the side and then turning around to run. Shelly had told them the detectives knew enough not to put their finger on the trigger, but the average attacker wouldn't anticipate her fighting back.

That move alone would have broken his finger. I shuddered at the thought.

Eleni had barely moved off the mat when Shelly yelled, "Turning the Flame!"

Jaz jumped on the mat with a devilish look in her eye at her boyfriend. The next thing we saw, Boomer had moved behind her at lightning speed, with the same gun poking into her back this time.

"Put your hands up where I can see them," he growled, sounding menacing and scary and anything but playful.

"Okay, okay." Jaz snapped to attention and quickly thrust her hands in the air, making sure to keep them shoulder level, and glanced over her shoulder like we were taught to see which hand the gun was in. Then she spun around to face him with determination in her eyes, wrapping her right hand around his wrist and twisting in an unnatural direction as she stepped forward with her left foot and pushed her left hand down on the back of his elbow.

Since arms aren't meant to bend that way, Boomer had no choice but to drop to the floor or have his arm break. Once she had him down and vulnerable, she wrenched the gun from his hand and threw it aside once more, only this time she snap-kicked him in his cup a couple of times before running away again.

"Yes, girl!" I yelled. "Show him who's boss." I slapped a hand over my mouth. Where had that come from?

Shelly wasted no time calling out, "Rising Elbows!"

Detective Johnson replaced Boomer and gave chase toward Aunt Tasoula. She screamed and ran away, zigzagging as if trying to outrun a bullet, but Darnell wasn't a bullet. He easily caught her in seconds and wrapped his huge arms around her from behind in a tight bear hug. She looked around like she'd forgotten what to do and then went limp as if playing dead, her head hanging to the side with eyes closed and tongue sticking out.

"You're not a possum, Soula," Ma yelled. "Fight back." She gave her Jazz hands and a meaningful look.

With her arms pinned to her sides, Aunt Tasoula looked helpless, but then she seemed to remember her hands were free and looked as if the moves had come back to her. She planted her feet back on the ground and grabbed his hands with her own and held on tight, then lunged to the right in another sumo stance to throw him off balance as she slipped her left foot behind his and twisted her body to the left, tripping him. Tightening her core, she held her stance as he fell down hard to the mat.

"Opa!" Aunt Tasoula managed to shout. Out of breath and exhausted, she stood there panting with a huge smile on her face.

Shelly started clapping, looking impressed, and intense relief flooded through me. We were done. Relief and pure satisfaction filled me.

Darnell rolled to his feet and walked over towards the edge of the mat. "Good job, ladies." He wrapped his arm around Ma's shoulders in a hug.

"Oh, my, well thank you." She patted his massive forearm.

I suddenly realized Ma was the only one who hadn't gone. My gaze met Shelly's. She didn't need to say a word. Her devilish grin said it all.

Crossing Guard!

Darnell tightened his arm, and Ma let out another curse before reacting on instinct. She slipped her foot behind his, lifted her arm, and twisted to the side, easily tripping him as he fell back, landing hard on his hindquarters.

"Your mama didn't raise you right, young man. You should have better manners than that," Ma said on a huff.

I couldn't help but giggle.

"Yes, ma'am." Darnell slowly climbed to his feet while rubbing his behind.

"Thank you, Shelly," Nik said.

"I prefer to be known as the Terminator." She winked. "Great job, ladies. I'm so proud of you all. Don't forget to practice every day. Like anything else, if you don't use it, you will lose it."

We all thanked her.

"Anytime, and remember I'm just a phone call away if you need anything at all. As for you three." Shelly pointed at the detectives. "I better see you in my class next week. You're all getting soft."

"You sure you don't want to come back on the force?" Nik asked. "We could use you."

"Oh, I'll be back, all right. To kick your butts in the gym." She gave him one last jab in the arm. "Anything beyond that you couldn't handle."

CHAPTER 20

Who said being a detective was exciting?

I'd been sitting in my car for hours that evening, still riding the adrenaline high from our self-defense class. I was alone, watching Nik watch Lord knew who. Stake-outs were the most boring thing on the planet. If I had realized that, I would have brought some snacks. I was starving and hot because I didn't dare leave my car in case he heard me. I was positive he had seen something on that security video at the hotel. He hadn't said anything to me, and I hadn't asked. We were supposed to be sharing information, but obviously, this was something he wanted to keep to himself.

And I wanted to know why.

He had pulled over down the street around the corner from the park. I'd parked way down the road from him so he wouldn't see my Prius. It was kind of hard to miss since I was the only one in town who owned one. My eyes were so tired from staring at him, but I didn't want to miss anything. I rubbed my eyes and refocused, then sat up straight.

He'd gotten out of the car, and I'd nearly missed it.

I quietly climbed out of my own car and kept to the shadows.

A couple times he looked behind him, but I flattened myself against a building or ducked behind a boulder. The last of the pink, purple, and orange rays had faded from the sky, turning the area around the park dark with the exception of a few lamps near the park pavilion and parking lot. The park was closed now, so it should be deserted, but it was summer. Teenagers often hung out there after hours, or people up to no good.

Once again, I wondered what we were doing here.

Nik darted from one tree to the next, getting closer to the Pavilion. A movement drew my eyes forward beyond Nik. I couldn't quite make out what it was, so I took a risk and moved forward as well. I squinted to see better, and sucked in a sharp breath then slapped a hand over my mouth and ducked.

Nik looked behind him but didn't see me.

I peeked back up to make sure my eyes weren't fooling me. Sure enough, Thalia stood beneath the pavilion talking to Benny and Baldy this time. What on earth could they be talking about? I could hear their voices carry on the night air, but I couldn't make out their words. Thalia's hands flew about as she talked as if she were angry. Benny made an aggressive step toward her, and Thalia got in a ready stance like we'd learned in class, but then Baldy put a hand on Benny's shoulder and he stopped.

I hadn't even realized I'd lunged forward until a hand slipped over my mouth and flipped me on my back, then a body pressed down on top of me. Shoot. I'd made the biggest mistake of all in not being aware of my surroundings. I couldn't breathe and started to panic. Shelly was right. You had to practice because all my training went out the window. *Why don't you ever listen to me, you stubborn woman, now stop moving before they see us.*

I stilled instantly.

Detective Dreamy, thank the lord.

Finally, Nik rolled off of me and stared up at the stars. "What were you thinking, Ballas? It's a good thing I doubled back around you. What did you plan to do? Run after them and save her?"

I stayed on my back, catching my breath. "I don't know. I just knew I would be there for her if she needed me. We protect our own. You know that. It's what we've been taught since birth."

"Obviously you both need to practice." He grunted. "She's my cousin, Kalli. I wouldn't have let anything happen to her."

"I know." I reached over and held his hand, needing his touch at the moment.

He didn't let go.

"Why didn't you tell me you saw something in the video, and what does it have to do with Thalia?"

"How'd you know?"

I shrugged. "I guess I know *you*."

"The person in the video was tall and thin, but you couldn't tell if they were a man or a woman. Except one thing." He paused for a minute and then seemed to make up his mind about something. "The person wore a black hoodie. When they unlocked the hotel room door, I noticed a bleach spot on the cuff of the sleeve."

"Okay?" I looked at him.

He stared up at the sky, then closed his eyes. "I put that there."

"What do you mean?"

Opening his eyes, he rolled over to look at me, letting go of my hand as he propped himself up on his elbow. "Last Christmas, Thalia and I were helping her ma with her cleaning business to clean my uncle's restaurant for our family Christmas party, and I spilled bleach on her sleeve. She was so mad because it was her favorite sweatshirt."

"Oh, I see," I said, then his words sank in. "Oh, wow, I *see*."

"Exactly." He let out a troubled sigh, rolled onto his back again and took my hand once more. *What am I going to do?*

I let go of his hand and sat up. "Thalia is family." I peeked behind us and the three of them were gone. "There has to be a reason why she broke into Penelope's hotel room. I refuse to believe she's a murderer or a thief, but Penelope might."

"I can't hide evidence. I have to tell what I know." He sat up and helped me to my feet. "But first, I'm going to talk to my cousin and find out what's going on."

THE NEXT DAY, Nik and I tailed Thalia together. He knew I would probably follow him anyway, and he was afraid I would get hurt looking on my own. So, he'd given in and agreed to let me tag along.

"Where do you think she's going?" I asked.

"I used to think I knew my cousin," he mumbled, staying far enough back so she wouldn't see him. "Now I'm not so sure. I wouldn't put anything out of the realm of possibility after seeing her break into a hotel room."

"There has to be an explanation," I said, but wasn't sure who I was trying to convince more.

She drove around several streets as though making sure she wasn't being followed, but Nik was good at his job. He knew how to tail someone and not be seen. Finally, she pulled into Clearview Airport. The airport was a small airport on the outskirts of town.

"My relatives all drove into town when they helped Ma move into her new house. What is Thalia doing here?"

"I don't know anyone who flew into Clearview Airport." I tried to think of all the people who had attended the Precious Gems and Jewelry Fair. "Most people from far away fly into a bigger airport because this small one can't handle the big planes."

"Benny and Tedesco are within driving distance, so they wouldn't have flown. Neither would Penelope or Ariana." He shut off the car. "Only one way to find out." He climbed out of the car only after Thalia had left hers.

Not about to be left behind, I quickly followed him.

We made our way inside the small airport and looked around the main hub. I didn't see her, so we started walking around. Rounding the corner, we came to a wall of lockers. There was Thalia, looking through a box she had pulled out of a locker and set on a bench. She pulled out an item then dropped it on the floor and stomped on it with her shoe. Picking it up, she tossed it back in the box.

"What the heck did she do that for?" I asked, totally confused.

"Most airports have lockers people can store things in for up to ninety days. The real question is what on earth does Thalia have that she has to store in secret away from the family and now break?" Nik asked, obviously not really expecting an answer.

I just followed along in silence.

I could feel the tension increase in the air around us. Nik was vibrating with frustration and anger. This wasn't going to be good.

"I'm only going to ask you this one more time, Thalia," Nik said in a voice I didn't quite recognize.

She looked up in shock, her face draining of color.

"What is going on? And don't even think about lying to me again."

Her shoulders wilted and tears filled her eyes as she dropped down onto the bench beside the box. "I can't take it anymore."

I started to go to her, but Nik shot me a look that said stay put. I clasped my hands in front of me and didn't move because it was a family matter. And, like it or not, this wasn't my family or my place to interfere.

"What can't you take anymore?"

"The blackmail."

He frowned, his jaw hardening. "Who is blackmailing you?"

"First it was Ariana, and now it's Benny."

"Why do you have things in a locker at the airport?"

"It's not my locker," she admitted and held up a key. "I found this hidden in a secret compartment of her little black book when I broke into her hotel room, which I'm sure you figured out, and that's why you're here." She puckered her brow. "How did you find out, anyway? I thought I was so careful."

"Bleach stain on your sleeve in the surveillance camera."

Recognition dawned in her eyes. "Last Christmas. Yup. I should have known that would come back to bite me in the backside."

"And I should have known Ariana had a black

book." Nik's shoulders wilted a little. No matter what Ariana had done, he had cared for her at one point. "Continue."

"I'm a realtor. I recognize an airport locker key when I see one. Back in the city, several of my clients would use them to store their luggage while house hunting. Ariana was a realtor as well. I'm sure she knew the same and realized this would be the perfect place to hide the video she was blackmailing me with."

"What happened, Thalia?"

"I was so naïve. At one time, I actually thought I was in love with Benny Balboa," she admitted, looking sick to her stomach. "He never loved me. He played me. I met him when I showed him a high-end penthouse, like the kind the stars stay in. I worked so hard to build my clientele. I wanted to impress him. I had no idea he was connected to the mob."

"Let me guess. He liked your connection to wealthy people." Nik clenched his jaw, and a muscle bulged.

"Bingo." She touched her nose. "I'm ashamed to admit it, but he seduced me in a mansion I was showing for my most famous client. What I didn't know is that he set up a video while I was in the bathroom and then he taped us."

"He wanted leverage over you so he could control you."

She nodded. "He never got the chance. Ariana stole him from me, and suddenly, she was doing his bidding. It was fine by me after I realized he was connected to the mob. But when they broke up, she was no fool. She found the video and took it with her. She was desperate. She knew you didn't just walk away from the mob, so she armed herself with anything she could for protection. I hate to say it, but I think she thought dating a cop would offer her even more protection."

Nik paused, as if letting that information digest, before asking, "How did you find out she had the video?"

"She tried to use it against me when she first got to town. Threatened to ruin my career unless I convinced you to marry her. But then Benny showed up unexpectedly, and she panicked. Soon after, she was dead."

"Do you know what Benny wanted from her?"

"I really don't. At first, I thought they were together, but then I realized he was blackmailing her, too. Then someone murdered her."

"Do you think Benny did it?"

"I wouldn't be surprised. I confronted him, and he threatened me with the video of us, but I called his bluff. That's why I broke into Penelope's motel room. I was looking for the video. When I found the hidden key, I knew I'd finally found it." She reached into the box and pulled out the video she had smashed. "I'm prepared to accept my fate. I can live with anything now that I know no one will ever see that video again."

"We'll get to that, but first, why were you in the park with Balboa and Tedesco?" Nik studied her carefully. He knew her so well; he would know if she was lying.

"You saw us?"

"I'm good at my job, Thalia." He sighed. "I don't want to see you get into trouble. I promise I'll help you as much as I can."

"I know you will, and I'm sorry for putting you in this position. I just want away from Benny once and for all."

"What did they want?"

"They were trying to get me to pick up where Ariana left off. Something about pawning fake jewelry. I said no, of course. That's why I wanted to learn self-defense, although, if the mob wants me gone, they'll find a way to make me disappear for good."

"I won't let that happen," Nik vowed. "Do you think they took Ma's heirloom necklace? Are they the Business Bandit?"

"I think they might be, but of course, Benny would never admit it to me. I did learn one thing last night."

"What's that?"

"Just because Balboa and Tedesco are working together doesn't mean they're friends. Benny came to Clearview after Ariana for some reason, and Antonio Tedesco came to Clearview after Benny. I heard them arguing, and Antonio said, *'you owe me'* and *'someone's gotta pay.'* Then he said something about Benny would be wise not to make him have to take action again, whatever that means."

"Thanks, Thalia. You've been a big help. I have to tell Penelope Drakos about you being the one who broke into her hotel room. It's my job."

"I know, and I don't blame her if she presses charges. I'm just glad the blackmailing is over with." She handed the broken video to Nik.

"The way I see it, it's inadmissible now." He handed it back to her with a wink. "As for Penelope, I don't think she will press charges. She's a Greek. Our family and Kalli's family are helping her. She hates Benny Balboa most of all. Hopefully, with your tip, Benny Balboa is finally going down."

CHAPTER 21

The next day the bells over the front door of Full Disclosure chimed and in walked Antonio Tedesco, looking like a Non-jolly Bald Giant. I sucked in a breath and ducked behind my mannequin from my perch up in the loft.

"Good morning, sir," I heard Jaz say from the store below. "May I help you with anything today?"

I peeked over the top of the railing.

Antonio looked around and said, "Just browsing," in that super deep baritone voice of his. "I'll know what I'm looking for when I see it." As if drawn to me, his gaze suddenly shot up to mine and locked. "Found it."

My heart dropped to my toes.

Jaz looked up at me with wide eyes.

Antonio started walking toward the stairs.

"Oh, sir, you can't go up there. That's not part of the store, it's just a work space for my partner." She hustled after him, but he ignored her and kept walking. "Should I call someone, Kalli?"

"It's okay, Jaz," I said, thrusting out my chin and refusing to show how terrified I was. "He can come up." I tried to act like he didn't bother me at all, but that didn't mean I wasn't planting my feet in a ready position and mentally rehearsing moves.

"Well, I'll be right down here within earshot if you need anything," she said loudly. "Just holler at me."

"Will do," I said and stepped back from the railing.

"Thank you for seeing me, Ms. Ballas," he said when he reached the top of the stairs, blocking out everything below.

Antonio was a very large man. Almost as big as Detective Johnson. He wore a black suit, tailored to perfection, a watch that cost more than my car, and a ring the *size* of my car. There wasn't a single strand of hair on his head or body that I could see or a spec of lint on his clothes. I appreciated the Mr. Clean look, but when he ignored my hand sanitizer stand and walked around the loft, touching pieces of lace and satin, it made my fingers itch to wash the material immediately.

"What can I do for you, Mr. Tedesco?" I clasped my hands together in front of me to keep from fidgeting.

"I was thinking of having a piece designed for my lady back home."

"I can do that," I said suspiciously, my Spidey senses going off. I didn't trust a word that came out of his mouth. "What are thinking of?"

"I'm looking for a unique, one-of-a-kind heirloom quality piece." His eyes shot to mine, locked, and held them captive. "Would you happen to have anything like that around, maybe up here?"

"No, I would not." I crossed my arms over my chest. "When would you need this heirloom piece by?"

"People who know me, know that I'm an impatient

man. I'm working on that." His eyes held no emotion, looking flat and lifeless, belying his words. He was probably an amazing poker player. "The sooner the better would be much appreciated."

"I'll see what I can do." I refused to be intimidated. "When did you say you were leaving?"

"I didn't." He brushed non-existent lint off his jacket. "That all depends on when I finish conducting my business in Clearview."

"Oh? And what business would that be?" I tapped my foot three times. "The jewelry business?"

His hands stilled.

"I saw you at the Precious Gems and Jewelry Fair, remember?" I smiled at him all innocent like.

"Ah, yes. You ran into me, and I told you to be careful. That I wouldn't want to see you get hurt." His gaze met mine and held once more. "The warning still stands, given the danger around town as of late." His tone was soft.

His eyes were not.

The bells over the front door chimed once more. We broke eye contact and both looked over the railing. In walked Detective Matheson. He handed Jaz a cup of coffee and a bag of goodies, spoiling her as usual, then kissed her cheek.

"Everything okay?" he asked.

"I'm fine, Kalli's fine, everything's fine, couldn't be better," she blurted. "Why do you ask?"

"You have a strange look on your face. And you always ramble when you're nervous." He looked around, his gaze stopping and narrowing as Antonio and I walked down the stairs. "Morning, Tedesco. Can't imagine what you're doing in my girlfriend's boutique. Please, enlighten me."

"He commissioned a Kalli Original from me," I

said and then turned to Antonio. "I will come up with some designs and get back to you. How can I reach you?"

He handed me his business card. "I look forward to doing business with you, Ms. Ballas." He tipped his head to Jaz, his gaze landing on Boomer. "Detective."

I watched him leave then slumped forward, letting out a huge breath of air I hadn't realized I'd been holding.

"What was that about?" Boomer asked.

"Keeping my enemies closer," I said, walking out the door.

"Where are you going?" Jaz hollered after me.

"To take another shower. I suddenly feel dirty."

"Thanks for picking me up," I said to Nik after I finished scrubbing my skin off in the shower. He'd brought me to my parents' restaurant for a minute, and now we were headed to the community center.

Boomer had given me a ride home earlier because someone had slashed my tires. I could only imagine who that someone was, but I couldn't prove it. Jaz didn't have cameras that reached the entire back parking lot. They focused on the back door and the building itself. I always parked at the edge of the parking lot to save room for the customers.

Not anymore.

"Boomer called me and filled me in after he dropped you off at home and had your car towed to the shop." Nik's jaw tightened. "You don't really think he wants lingerie from you, do you?"

"No, he was warning me to butt out of his business

or else. The tires were a little display of what *or else* might mean."

"I don't want you going anywhere alone until he leaves town." Nik's knuckles were white as he gripped the steering wheel. The fine lines at the corners of his eyes were deeper than normal, looking like he hadn't gotten much sleep as of late.

I touched his arm. "I won't, I promise."

He took a deep breath, held it, then exhaled slowly until his muscles relaxed. "I can't handle losing anyone else I care about," he finally said. *Especially not you.*

I squeezed once then let go of his arm. "You won't."

Nik pulled into the community center. Pop and Papou were at their weekly Scrabble Club meeting. Ma had asked me to drop off a tray of Mosaiko—Greek chocolate and biscuits mixed together into a loaf she sliced.

"You know, Baldy's words keep coming back to me," I said, having relived everything that had happened this morning.

"How so?" Nik looked at me curiously.

"I don't think he or Benny stole your ma's necklace."

His eyebrows drew together. "Why not?"

"He kept hinting around when describing what he was looking for in *lingerie* that he wanted something unique. Heirloom worthy. He definitely wasn't talking about lingerie. I think he was fishing to see if I knew where the necklace really was. Maybe they think we made up the theft as a cover to keep the necklace safe."

"That wouldn't have been a bad idea. Too bad we didn't think of it before it actually did get stolen, and I'm no closer to figuring out who the real Bandit is."

Nik opened his door and took the dessert tray from the back seat.

"You don't have to carry that in for me."

"I don't mind, Ballas." His gaze softened. "I like doing things for you." He looked away and started walking to the community center door. "You know. As friends," he said over his shoulder, shooting me another wink before facing front once more.

"Right. Friends." Why had I made that rule? I followed him with my eyes, watching his muscles dance as he walked, and I sighed with regret. If the man knew what a single wink from him did to me, he would be relentless in his pursuit of me.

Nik stepped through the door, and I paused outside. He hesitated, looking back over his shoulder.

"Go on ahead. I'll catch up. My shoe came undone."

He nodded and kept walking while I bent down to tie my sneakers. I didn't plan on going back to work today, so I'd donned a short outfit and sneakers, intending to go for a walk after finishing my errand for my ma. I stood up and put my hand on the door, when that same sensation that I was being watched made the hairs on my head stand out like Prissy's calico coat did when Wolfgang got too close.

I let go of the door and spun around. Again, no one was there. The door opened behind me, and I jumped.

"You okay?" Nik asked, looking at me with concern.

"Yes, sorry. My imagination is running away with me once again. Go figure." I laughed a little too loud. "Thanks again for the ride."

"Anytime." He leaned in and kissed my cheek, surprising me, then he winked and walked away, leaving me wondering if he could suddenly read *my* mind.

I touched my cheek while the butterflies danced in my stomach once more. Looking around warily one last time, I headed inside. The room was filled with both men and women who loved the game of scrabble.

Pop and Papou sat at a table across from each other while Rex Drummond and Michael Flannigan played their own game at a table right next to them.

"Hey, Pop, how's the Mosaiko?" I stood by my father.

"I married the best cook in three counties," he said with pride, rubbing his slightly rounded belly.

"Second to YiaYia, of course." Papou nodded, letting out a sigh of satisfaction.

"Of course," I agreed, leaning in to kiss his cheek. "Ma learned from the best." I gave him a quick squeeze then let go.

"I wish someone would teach Lois a thing or two." Michael snorted. "Trust me when I say I didn't marry my wife for her cooking."

I glanced at Rex who was three shades of red. "Best dessert I've ever had," he managed to say and actually met my gaze. "Tell your mother and grandmother we said thank you. It's much appreciated."

Progress.

"I will just as soon as I see her. You gentleman have fun. I'm gonna grab Ma's dish and head out the back. It's a beautiful day for a walk." I waved to them then made my way to the kitchen.

Ma's dish was empty, not even crumbs left. I chuckled. I washed the dish and dried it, then tried the back door. It was locked. Oh well, I would just have to go out the front. I started to head through the kitchen door, but that was locked too.

"Okay, that's strange."

I knocked, but no one heard. The noise of people shouting when they won and arguing when they didn't, drowned out my pitiful knock on a door in the back of the building. I reached for my phone in my back pocket. Closing my eyes, I realized I'd set it on the counter in the restaurant when I'd picked up Ma's dessert.

Someone had to notice I was missing eventually.

At least the kitchen had appliances, basic supplies and a table. I wouldn't starve to death and would just have to deal with the recycled air from the air conditioning. I sat down and waited. What was that smell? I frowned and sniffed. My eyes widened. I went over and checked the stove to make sure everything was turned off. It was. And the microwave was unplugged.

Then why did I smell smoke?

I looked all around the room, but I couldn't find the source. It suddenly dawned on me. It wouldn't matter how many supplies I had if I were dead...

The community center was on fire!

CHAPTER 22

The smoke alarm went off, and I could hear everyone scrambling to leave the building. The only problem was...everyone thought I had already gone home. I started screaming and pounding on the door, but no one seemed to hear.

This was no good, as Ma and Aunt Thalia would say.

The smoke started seeping in under the door. I'd read somewhere that you should wet a towel and put it along the crack. Running to the sink, I found a couple dish towels. I soaked them and then ran back to shove them under the door. I yanked my hand away.

The door was already hot.

Looking around, I started to panic. I didn't want to die by smoke inhalation, or heaven forbid, burning up in a fire. The kitchen didn't have a window, and the back door was still locked. I started pounding on the back door, harder this time, and screaming for all I was worth. My life started to flash before my eyes. What if I died and never gave Nik a chance? He didn't know how I felt about him.

Why had I said I just wanted to be friends?

Regret filled every cell in my body. Had I told my parents how grateful I was that they had adopted me? How much I loved them? And Jaz. The thought of never seeing my best friend again made me cry. Tears streamed down my face when I heard the noise. It sounded like banging. Was I hallucinating? Lord only knew what the smoke was doing to the inside of my body.

"Kalli? Are you in there?" said a male voice.

I knew that voice!

"Yes, Max, I'm in here!" I yelled.

Max was an EMT and a firefighter. We grew up together. He used to have a thing for me but backed off when he realized I only liked him as a friend. Now he dated Eleni's boyfriend's sister, Marigold, who was a voodoo practicing Romani woman. If I found out who locked me in here, I was going to have her put a curse on them. If my hunch was right, Mr. Clean's head would be smoking by the time I was done with him.

"Kalli, stand back away from the door. I'm going to get you out."

"Okay," I yelled and moved back." The door going into the rest of the community center snapped and crackled as the fire ate its way through the wood. "Hurry," I added, moving away from that door as well.

Max started hacking away at the door with an axe. He chopped and sliced and the door finally flew open just as the other door came crashing down in flames. I didn't hesitate. I ran through the open door and out to the back of the building.

Bursting into tears, I ran straight into Nik's open arms.

He held me and didn't say a thing, but his thoughts mirrored mine. *Oh, baby, if I had lost you, I seriously don't know what I would do.* His arms tightened, and I snuggled in deeper, craving to stay in his arms which I hadn't thought possible with anyone not too long ago. I was in awe of how he made me feel. He was the only human being on this planet who could make me get out of my own head. I had to show him at least a little bit of how I was feeling.

I leaned back, wrapped my arms around his neck, and kissed his lips. He held me tighter and kissed me back.

Everyone cheered, which had us breaking apart and laughing. I looked around. Literally everyone was there. My family. Nik's family. Pretty much the entire town, except Benny and Baldy, of course. I was sure they were hiding out somewhere close by, watching their handiwork. Once people had heard the sirens and found out the community center was on fire, they'd come running.

"How did you guys know I was in there?" I asked Max, who insisted on checking me out the second that Nik had let me go.

Max jerked his head to the side where Erik and my cousin Yanni were talking. "You got lucky. The community center is one of Yanni's accounts, so Erik was here mowing and saw the smoke. He heard you yell, and he called 911 immediately."

"I owe that man. I wonder if he saw anything? I'll be right back," Nik said and left to go talk to him. Boomer, Darnell, and Captain Crenshaw joined him along with Fire Chief Rebecca Giddings and Mayor Riboldazzi.

"Am I gonna live?" I asked Max.

"I'm beginning to wonder that myself," he teased.

I waved off his hands. "All right, all right. I'm fine, but don't tell Doc, or I'll have your girlfriend put a voodoo curse on *you*." I gave him a fake scowl while he held his hands up and backed away with mock horror on his face.

I turned around and headed toward the inevitable. Pop, Papou, Rex and Michael were all talking with the rest of the Scrabble Club members, probably about where their next meeting was going to be held. Lois was talking with Chloe and Penelope, shaking their heads and looking upset. Meanwhile, the women in my life spotted me and came running.

"I should have known when you locked yourself in the bathroom as a child, you were no good with the lock." Ma inspected every inch of me.

Aunt Tasoula picked up a strand of my hair and smelled it. "The smoke is strong within you. You come by. I wash it with aloe."

Jaz hugged me hard. "Don't you scare me like that again." She let go and gave me a look that said, *Trust me, you don't want to hear my thoughts right now*.

"Ditto," Eleni said.

"Yeah, we've had enough drama in this town," Thalia added, glancing over at Penelope and looking ashamed. Penelope hadn't pressed charges after hearing the whole story, but she still wasn't happy with her.

"Stop, drop, roll. Stop, drop, roll," Frona sang while she did somersaults across the lawn, got up and pointed, adding, "Baldy stopped, his car dropped, and now he's rolling down the street in the heat while Kalli nearly burned her feet."

My head whipped up and I stared at the street, locking eyes with Antonio Tedesco and Benny Balboa. Antonio stared at me until the end of the road, then Benny saluted as they rounded the corner out of sight.

~

Jaz and I sat on our deck, having a drink later that night.

"I can't believe you nearly died." Jaz crossed her bare feet at the ankles on top of a footstool. "My best friend nearly burned to a crisp. I will never eat anything deep-fried again." She shuddered.

"Thanks for the visual." I sat in the Adirondack chair next to her with my legs curled pretzel style in my seat, and Prissy in my lap. She hadn't left my side since I'd returned. I'd showered, but I wondered if she could smell smoke on my insides or something, which kind of freaked me out. "I can't figure it out," I added, trying to distract myself. "I didn't lock myself in the kitchen. I never touched the lock after I entered." I wrapped my arms around my cat. "Someone definitely locked me in and set the fire intentionally, knowing I was in there." My eyes met hers. "Someone tried to kill me."

"This craziness seriously needs to stop."

"You're telling me. If Doc LaLone knew I was having a glass of wine after breathing in smoke, he would probably suggest an intervention and send me to the funny farm." Now that I thought about it, I set my glass of chardonnay down, worrying if I'd done any permanent damage.

"I thought you said not much smoke had filled the room before Max got you out?" She tilted her head.

I shrugged. "It didn't."

"Then drink up, sister." She held her glass in the air. "I think your nerves are in worse shape than your lungs." She took a sip of her margarita. "I know mine are."

"Probably true." I picked my glass back up. "I have

my suspicions on who tried to kill me. Benny and Baldy drove right by the community center in broad daylight. I'm sure they were disappointed their fire didn't kill me."

"Why would they want to kill you?"

"Because they know I'm onto them. I'm figuring this case out, and they don't want that. If I'm no good to them, then I'm expendable, right? Isn't that how the mob works?"

"I don't like this one bit." A gust of wind blew leaves off a tree into our back yard. "I wonder when the guys will get back?" Jaz asked, searching the area warily.

"I have no clue. Knowing our men, they won't come home until they figure out what happened at the community center."

"*Our* men?" Jaz grinned, her wariness all but vanished.

"I know I said I only wanted to be Nik's friend, but after nearly dying in a fire, I've come to the conclusion I don't want to be Nik's friend. I want to be his girlfriend. I just have to inform him of that." I laughed.

"Um, I think he knows." She laughed with me. "I kind of figured it was an unspoken truth when I saw you two kissing."

"Correction. I kissed him. Yes, he kissed me back, but what guy wouldn't respond to a woman kissing him?" I took a sip of chardonnay.

"Girl, that man is crazy about you. Everyone can see that." She took a big drink of her margarita. "You just have to decide what you want and go for it."

"I know what I want. I'm just afraid because I said things were too complicated for him because of Ariana, that maybe now he will think things are too complicated for me because I have people trying to kill me."

"You're overthinking this. You said you've heard his thoughts. You know how he feels about you."

"Yes, but he hasn't expressed those feelings out loud." I set Prissy down and stood up to walk over to the railing and look out over our meticulous lawn. I glanced into Nik's yard and was pleased it was mowed and weeded to perfection. Good boy. He'd kept up using my cousin's lawn service. At least that was something.

"He hasn't had a chance to express himself, Kalli." Jaz got up and joined me, glancing up at the overcast sky, and not from an impending storm. The fire had created a layer of haze that blocked out the stars. "Look. You like him, and he likes you. He's the first man who has actually made you get out of your head. That alone deserves a second chance." She squeezed my hand. "Remember, he can't read *your* mind. You need to tell him how you feel. Give whatever this is between you two a real shot."

"You're right. I'm overthinking things as usual."

"I took your advice last time, and look at where I am with Boomer. The man still drives me crazy, but I can't imagine life without him now." She tipped her glass back and emptied it. "And that scares the starch right out of me."

A noised sounded in the woods behind our fence.

Prissy sat up from her perch on the railing and hissed at the darkness. Wolfgang barked in response, racing around Nik's half of the yard, on alert. Another rustling sounded. What the heck was happening now?

My cell phone that Ma had returned to me after I didn't burn up in a fire rang. I checked the caller I.D. and answered.

"Nik? Where are you?" There was a pause on the line, and Jaz and I looked at each other. "What's wrong?"

"While everyone was distracted by the fire, another break-in happened."

Jaz's eyes widened. She could hear him through my phone. I put it on speaker so she could hear better. "Where?"

"Full Disclosure," Nik said, adding with satisfaction in his voice, "but this time we caught the Business Bandit red handed."

I closed my eyes then looked at Jaz who was already heading into the house. Good thing I had hardly touched my wine. "We're on our way."

CHAPTER 23

"I knew it!" I said as Jaz and I walked through the front door of Full Disclosure and saw the guilty culprits.

Benny Balboa and Antonio Tedesco were in handcuffs, seated on Jaz's couch while Detective Stevens, Detective Matheson, and Detective Johnson questioned them.

"You don't know anything," Benny said.

"I know we don't have to say anything until our lawyer gets here." Baldy glared at me. "You don't know who you're messing with, little girl."

"Knock it off," Nik growled. "You're just mad because you got caught in the act. You set the fire as a distraction to draw the whole town out so you could hit up another business. Unfortunately for you, your plan backfired."

"You got sloppy, boys," Boomer chimed in. "Your biggest mistake was messing with my girlfriend."

Jaz joined us after inspecting her entire boutique from top to bottom. "It doesn't look like they took anything."

"Because we caught them before they could,"

Boomer stated. "It was only a matter of time before they made a mistake."

"I told you we're not the thieves." Benny shook his head, giving Nik a look of disgust. "You're the one who's sloppy."

"Looks to me like you're the one who messed up, Balboa," Darnell chimed in. "My sources tell me Ariana stole drugs from your apartment when she dumped you, and then she sold them for enough money to skip town. That had to make you furious." He studied him. "Furious enough to kill, even."

"I didn't kill her. We might have broken up, but I wouldn't want her to die. I just wanted the drug money, except she spent it all." His jaw hardened.

"The drugs weren't hers or yours, were they?" Nik said calmly. "They belonged to the Tedesco Family, and now they want their money."

"You don't know what you're talking about," Benny spat.

"Oh, I think I do," Nik went on. "You caught up with Ariana and threatened to turn her over to the mob. Why didn't you?"

"Stupid broad said she could get your mother's heirloom necklace. She figured it was worth something, but none of us knew just how much it would be worth," Antonio ground out. "Amateurs. I never should have let them make the plan. It was Benny's dumb idea to fake a pregnancy to get you to marry her."

"The idea wasn't dumb," Benny growled back. "She always liked me more than him. She never planned to marry him. She just needed to get close enough to steal the necklace."

"She's dead," Antonio pointed out dryly. "I'd say that makes the idea pretty stupid. She got what she deserved for crossing my family." He leaned forward. "You know the rules, Benny. Someone's gotta pay for the stolen drugs."

"Is that why you were pawning the fakes?" Boomer asked. "That idea wasn't much better. You ticked off some powerful people who will want a piece of you, but they will have to wait in line. You're going to jail."

"If he makes it there alive," Antonio said with a deep deadly tone and a look in his eye that sent shivers across my flesh.

"I wouldn't look so smug, Tedesco. You're joining him," Nik pointed out with relish, the look in *his* eye one of pure satisfaction.

"We'll see about that. I have powerful people of my own."

I had gone upstairs to check out the loft as they talked and came back down. "Why did you ransack my studio?"

Baldy's hard eyes settled on me, and I tried not to squirm. "I told you to be careful, little girl. I always get what I want."

"Not this time, pal." Darnell hoisted Baldy to his feet because he was the only one big enough to do so.

"I got this one," Boomer said, grabbing Benny and pulling him to his feet. "You messed with the wrong business. It's gonna be a pleasure taking you to your new home."

"I'll meet you guys at the station," Nik said.

The detectives left, and I breathed a sigh of relief. "I'm glad that's over. Antonio killed Ariana for crossing his family. He hit me over the head at your ma's place, looking for the necklace. He locked me in a building and set it on fire. I don't think he would have stopped until I was dead."

"I'm afraid he killed Nina as well. We found her

journal saying she was going to apologize to Ma for threatening her about dating Captain Crenshaw. She must have shown up when Ma was sleeping and caught Antonio there, so he killed her before she could turn him in." Nik breathed out a heavy sigh. "He's not saying where the necklace is. I have a feeling they pawned that right away. We'll most likely never see that again."

"Why mess with my loft if they already had the necklace?" I hated the thought of him violating my private sanctuary. I would have to do a thorough cleaning before I would feel comfortable up there again.

"Antonio likes to send a message. He already told you to back off, but you didn't listen. He didn't like that."

"I know. I felt his presence following me every day."

"I'm sure he didn't expect to get caught before they finished. It was a fluke that the boys and I were out looking for leads from the fire when we spotted Antonio's black sedan hidden in an alley down the street. We went on foot and saw a dim flashlight in the loft window of Full Disclosure. I knew it wasn't you or Jaz, and we were able to surprise them in the act. You don't have to worry about either of them anymore." He hugged me. "We're good at our jobs, Kalli. We'll get them to confess to the rest. It's over, Babe." *Now maybe we can finally get our lives back on track.*

A little thrill zipped through me over the word *Babe*. I'd never been anyone's Babe, or any other term of endearment, and I kind of liked it. "Nothing has ever sounded better," I admitted, then took a chance and added, "You still owe me a date, Detective."

He froze, then leaned back to look me in the eye. "You sure?" *Please be sure.*

I stood on my tiptoes and kissed him in answer. *Finally, something is going right.*

～

THE NEXT DAY, I told Nik I would drop Wolfgang off at Dino's Doggy Daycare for him. He and the other detectives had their hands full, wrapping up the case. Chloe was packing in preparation to move back into her own house.

Life was finally good.

I fed Prissy, said goodbye to Chloe, and walked Wolfgang to my car. Nik had put down a waterproof seat protector in the back, which helped, but I would still need another detail done before I could sleep at night. I put Wolf in the back seat as Rex pulled up in his mail truck. I climbed in my car, and Wolf let out a low growl.

"Oh, you big goofball," I said, as I pulled out of the driveway and waved to Rex. "Trust me, he's harmless." Rex stared at me a little less red faced, then waved back and moved on down the street to the next house.

Progress.

I arrived at Dino's Doggy Daycare and dropped off Wolfgang. As I came back out, I ran into Milly with Elenore and Olivia's full-grown poodles. They were gorgeous dogs, jet black with the blingiest of collars I'd ever seen. I chuckled.

"Guess what?" she said breathlessly.

I couldn't help but smile over her excitement. "What?"

"I took your advice and talked to Nelson."

"You did? That's wonderful. And...?"

"And what?" She blushed.

"Don't keep me in suspense." I laughed. "What happened?"

"Oh, well, no big deal. He asked me to go to a jewelry show with him today, is all. I'm sure he was just being friendly."

"That's amazing. When do you leave?"

"Oh, I'm not going." She waved me off with her hand.

"Milly," I waited until she looked me in the eye. "Why on earth would you say no when he asked you on a date?"

"I volunteer at the shelter, but I work at Dino's. My boss said I could take the rest of the day off, but I already promised the Bennett twins I would take their dogs, Chanel and Versace, to the park and then run them home after. Nelson will already be gone by then." She shrugged. "That's okay. At least we're talking. That's a start."

"Well, that's silly. It's a beautiful day, and I have nothing to do. I would be more than happy to do it for you."

"I couldn't let you. It's my job."

"If I can handle Wolfgang, I can handle any dog. I know the twins. They won't mind, I'm sure. At least go ask your boss. I'll wait here with Chanel and Versace as a little test. They're such darling divas."

The dogs sat like perfect little ladies, waiting for Milly to return. Five minutes later, Milly came running out of the daycare, all wide-eyed and red-faced with a huge smile.

"Dino said yes!" she squealed. "He called the twins and they were completely fine with you walking the girls and dropping them off. The fence to the back of the house is unlocked. They always just have me let the girls in there, but be sure to close the gate behind you when you leave so they won't get out."

"Done. Now go get your man."

She let out an excited giggle. "I already called him. He's waiting for me." She chewed her bottom lip. "Do I look okay?" She spun in a circle, wearing average shorts and a t-shirt with her hair in a ponytail. Nothing fancy, but it suited her.

If I'd learned anything about dating, you had to be yourself or it would never work. "You look adorable. From one overthinker to another, stop worrying and just go."

"You're right. Okay. Here I go." She ran to her car, took a deep breath, then jumped in and left.

I looked down, and the dogs stared up at me patiently. Who would have thought I would ever become a dog person? Well, not exactly a dog person, but at least one who could tolerate them now. "Okay, ladies, let's go."

The temperature was in the eighties with low humidity and not a cloud in the sky. I walked past businesses, waving to all the people I knew. Chanel and Versace were so well-trained they had a loose leash the whole way to the park. We stopped by Mr. Chew's ice cream stand for a couple of doggy bowls, and then Mr. Fender's food truck for a couple of dog treats he kept in there—reserving the hotdogs for Wolfgang. I was actually enjoying myself.

For the first time in weeks, I wasn't afraid.

Leaving the park, I headed back toward town and turned down the street the Bennett sisters' house was on. Rex was just putting their mail in the mailbox as I hit their driveway. He started to drive off, but stopped, backed up, and stuck his head out the window. "You just missed the sisters."

"That's okay. They said for me to put the dogs in the backyard, but thanks for letting me know."

He nodded once and then drove off to finish his route.

I opened the gate to the back fence and let the dogs in. Glancing around the yard, I was impressed. The rental house owners used my cousin's lawn service as well, and I was guessing Erik had done the landscaping. I was beginning to recognize his signature style.

"Aha, there you are." I saw the dog bowls on the deck.

There was plenty of shade in the yard, and the temperature outside wasn't too warm, but I didn't want to leave them without water in case the sisters were gone longer than they expected. I grabbed the bowls and filled them with water from the hose and then carried them back to the deck. The second I set them down, Chanel and Versace stuck their faces in them and drank deep, then plopped down in the shade to sleep.

"Good girls." I smiled, bending down to pat them on their heads, then I stood back up feeling like I'd really accomplished something.

I was about to leave for Dino's to pick up my car and go home when I noticed a trash bag on the floor by the trashcan in the kitchen through the sliding door. Tomorrow was trash day, so that wasn't surprising to see trash. The trash bag was clear, and what was inside *was* surprising. I tried to open the sliding door, but it was locked. Looking around, I noticed a window that was open to let in the breeze from the beautiful day.

I didn't hesitate.

I scrambled off the deck and made my way over to

the window. It was too high to reach, but I spotted a couple of Adirondack chairs. Putting one right beneath the window and standing on it, I was just able to reach the window. After some wiggling, I managed to get the screen out and pull myself through. The house was in immaculate order. Nothing seemed unusual except that trash bag.

Hurrying over to the bag and trying not to touch anything in case I was wrong, I looked closer through the bag. Sure enough, Aunt Tasoula's special night cream was in there. She'd ordered a paraben and petroleum jelly free cream with me in mind. No one had tried it yet because she had just gotten the shipment in when her salon was robbed.

I dropped the bag, my hands shaking as I backed away. Following my instincts, I quickly searched the rest of the house, becoming more and more shocked with each item I found.

The biggest item of all...the Pagonis family heirloom necklace.

Benny and Baldy weren't the Business Bandits. Elenore and Olivia Bennett were. I had to call Nik. I pulled out my phone when Chanel and Versace started barking. Making my way back to the kitchen, I started to open the sliding door to let them in, when an arm snaked around my shoulders.

This time I was prepared.

CHAPTER 24

I'd been practicing just like Shelly had taught us. I didn't have to think twice.

Crossing Guard!

The arm around my shoulders tightened, and I reacted on instinct just like Ma had in training. I slipped my foot behind my attacker's, lifted my arm, and twisted to the side, easily tripping the person as they fell back, landing hard on their hindquarters. I couldn't believe my eyes.

"Rex Drummond?" I gaped. "What are you doing here?"

He gingerly sat up. "I could ask you the same."

"I asked you first." Strange how he didn't blush or seem nervous in the least anymore. He was like a completely different person.

"Following you, if you must know." He rolled to his feet with ease.

I stepped back in a ready stance. "Stay where you are," I ordered, glancing around and spotting an empty bottle of Ouzo. I snatched it and held it high. I still needed to call Nik, but my phone had dropped to the floor when Rex grabbed me.

He held his hands out in front of him, palms up so I could see them. "I only grabbed you to keep you from letting the dogs in. Let me explain."

Suddenly, the front door lock turned.

"No time for that now. Hide," he said and ducked around the corner faster than I'd thought possible, and definitely faster than any mailman I'd ever seen.

I frowned. Who was this guy? Before I could ask, the front door opened. Elenore and Olivia walked in, carrying their mail.

"Kalli, what are you still doing here?" Eleanor asked, setting her bag of groceries down. "And inside our house? Our instructions were to leave the girls in the yard."

Olivia tossed the mail on the kitchen table. "And why are our dogs barking?" Her eyes widened at the bottle of Ouzo still in my hands.

I gripped the bottle tighter. "I know who you are. I saw my aunt's special night cream in your trash."

"Your aunt has wonderful products, dear." Eleanor walked toward me. "You know we love to shop."

"More like you love to steal. That product is new. My aunt hadn't sold it to anyone before the Business Bandit or should I say Bandits stole it." I raised the bottle higher and took a step back.

"Oh, dear," Olivia said. "And we really liked you." She rolled up her sleeves and walked towards me as well. "Such a shame. Maybe we can work out a deal."

"I saw the sleeping pills on your nightstand. I know you killed Ariana. And I found the heirloom necklace. I can't believe you killed the poor widow as well."

"We might be thieves, dear, but we're not killers. Give us some credit." Eleanor moved to the left, not missing a beat or seeming ruffled at all.

"We have class. Killers are thugs like those mobsters that were arrested. They are your killers. We just took advantage of the distraction they created. You can't fault us for capitalizing on their stupidity." Olivia moved to the right in a perfectly choreographed dance, as if they'd done this before.

They were surrounding me, blocking my escape.

I waved the bottle around. "Then what do you plan to do with me now that I know who you are? Let me walk away? I doubt it. You're going to kill me, too, aren't you?"

"Don't be silly. Your family really is so dramatic, dear. We'll simply lock you up while we move on to another town," Eleanor said, picking up a poker from the fireplace. "Now, be a good girl and don't make me use this. I really don't want to hurt you." She smiled pleasantly as if we were having tea. "I'm stronger than I look."

"Yes, fighting is so unbecoming of a lady," Olivia added, brushing the wrinkles out of her blouse. "I really liked Clearview, but we've outstayed our welcome. Time to change our names and find another gem of a town to harvest. You get her in the storage closet, Sister, and lock the door. I'll get the valuables, and we'll be gone within the hour."

"No one is going anywhere, and the only one who will get hurt is whoever doesn't listen to me," Rex said in a voice full of authority.

The sisters swung toward him, shock transforming their faces as they saw the gun he held in his hand pointed directly at them.

"Who are you?" I asked, confusion swirling through me.

"FBI Special Agent Harry Mulroney." He held up

an official badge while still wearing his mailman uniform.

I clapped my hands. "Well played, Harry. You certainly had me fooled."

He winked at me. Actually winked. My jaw fell open. This was not the Rex I knew, and I doubted Special Agent Harry had any trouble finding women.

"Ladies, put your hands in the air. If you'll turn around and face the wall, I would be much obliged."

They did as he said without protest, still appearing in shock.

After they were handcuffed and sitting on their couch, Harry called lord knew who and finally faced me. "Sorry for all the shenanigans, Ms. Ballas. I was playing a role and needed to stay in character."

"That's what I don't understand. Why would the FBI be after a couple of thieves in Clearview, Connecticut?"

"These aren't just any thieves. They're pros. They have been at this for over a decade across several state lines. They don't rob things like big banks that make the news. They simply strike smaller businesses to supply their style of living. I've been working on this case undercover for years, from town to town. They never wear the items they steal in the town they stole them in."

"What tipped you off this time," I asked, fascinated and still stunned, frankly.

"I followed a hunch this time and got lucky. When I saw them wearing items they stole from the last town they raided, I suspected it was them. But when I saw you drop their dogs off, I got worried you would blow this case by spooking them, and they would move on. They almost did. I'm glad I doubled back and followed you inside."

"I knew stealing that heirloom necklace would be our downfall," Eleanor said. "You always want more, Olivia. This is all your fault."

"That necklace would have set us up for the rest of our lives. One big job and we could have retired in style like we've always dreamed of." Olivia pouted.

"You'll be set up for the rest of your lives in a nice penitentiary," Rex aka Harry said as the sirens grew closer.

Neither rain, nor snow, nor sleet, nor hail shall keep the postmen—or the FBI apparently—from doing their jobs.

~

"That's the last of your things from my place, Ma." Nik set a box down in the kitchen. We'd spent all day moving Chloe back into her new house.

"I love you, my son, but's it good to have a place of my own." She patted his hand. "And now that my name is cleared, I might forgive your captain after all."

"I don't need to hear that, Ma." Nik held his hands up and backed away. "Are you sure you don't mind if I leave Wolf in the back yard?"

"He's fine," Chloe said with an adoring smile. "He misses his YiaYia, and let's face it. He might be the only grandchild I get. Just leave him tied up. We'll turn him loose when Erik finishes the lawn."

Nik looked at me and rolled his eyes then kissed the top of my head. "Call me if you need me. I'm off to the station to tie up loose ends with Special Agent Mulroney." He scratched his head. "That is one twist I didn't see coming."

"You and me both," I responded and blew him a kiss, feeling giddy as I watched him walk out the door.

"He's going to marry you some day," Chloe said to me after Nik was out of earshot. She started unpacking as if she hadn't just blown my world wide open.

"How can you say that? We're only planning our first official date," I sputtered, opening a box myself, needing something to do with my hands.

"Mamas know these things. Trust me. My son has *never* looked at a woman the way he looks at you."

An engine started up, drowning out her words through the open window. I glanced outside. Saved by a weedwhacker. She gave me a knowing look but didn't say anything more. We unpacked for the next hour with the sound of yardwork and Chloe's humming the only noises. It was kind of nice. Finally, the yard grew quiet.

A knock sounded at the back door.

"Come on in, Erik," Chloe said. "The door's open."

"You're all set for another week, ma'am." Erik stepped inside and pulled off his hat, a bead of sweat on his forehead from the day's heat.

If he cut his hair and shaved his beard, he'd be a lot cooler, I thought, heading to the kitchen to grab a bottle of water from the refrigerator.

"Please, call me Chloe. Thank you for keeping up with the yard while I was away. It really looks great."

I handed him the water bottle. "Here, take this before you go. It certainly is a hot one out there."

His hand touched mine as he took it. "Thank you," he said with a smile. *But I'm not going anywhere until I finish this.*

I jerked my hand away.

He frowned. "Is something wrong, Ms. Ballas?" He took a drink from the water bottle, looking genuinely concerned. Maybe my gift had short circuited.

"I don't know. Is there?" I tested it as I eyed him while I backed away toward the counter where my cellphone was...and the knife set.

"Whatever is the matter with you, Kalli?" Chloe asked.

Erik just watched me, and my gut told me I was right about him.

"Who are you?" I asked, grabbing a knife from the set I'd just unpacked.

"Why that's Erik, Kalli." Chloe gaped at me as if I'd lost my mind. "I'm calling Doc LaLone."

She headed toward the phone but Erik grabbed her before she could reach it. "Drop the knife, Ms. Ballas," he sneered, transforming into someone I no longer recognized. Into the monster I'd felt through his thoughts.

"Erik, dear, you're hurting me." Chloe winced.

"I'll hurt you worse, if she doesn't put the knife down."

"Okay, relax," I said, setting the knife back on the counter slowly and moving my hand away.

"You relax. Leave your phone and sit down right there." He pointed to the kitchen table and chairs.

I kept my hands where he could see them as he shoved Chloe into the chair beside me. He kept himself between us and our only escape. The back door.

"What do you want, Erik?" Chloe asked with a tremble in her voice, looking absolutely stunned at the turn of events.

"Quit calling me Erik," he sneered.

"Then what would you have us call you?" I asked calmly, trying not to rile him further while I figured a way out of this mess.

"Gabe."

I sucked in a sharp breath. "Gabe Scarlatta?" He

was the inmate who had escaped months ago that Darnell had come to Clearview to tell Nik about.

Gabe narrowed his eyes to slits. "So that's why Detective Johnson was in town. I wondered if he or Stevens would recognize me, but neither one did." He stroked his beard and shook his long hair. "Then again I look different than I did five years ago. I've thought about my revenge on Stevens every day in that cell while planning my escape."

"What did my son ever do to you?"

"Locked me up and ruined my life." His eyes turned sad. "I didn't mean to almost kill my wife, but she wouldn't listen. I only meant to rough her up a little and teach her a lesson. I tried explaining that to Stevens, but he wouldn't listen, either."

"Is that why you killed Ariana?" I asked, trying not to let my fear show. "Because she wouldn't listen, either?"

His eyes hardened again. "I *meant* to kill her to punish Stevens. You really should lock your doors." He looked at Chloe. "I followed her and caught her spying on you through the window. She waited until you stepped out of the room, then she put your sleeping pills into the bottle of alcohol and hid until you took it upstairs and passed out in bed."

"She was looking for your heirloom necklace," I said.

"I didn't care what she was looking for. I slipped upstairs without her knowing and snagged the bottle of alcohol. I wanted to hurt Stevens even more by killing his fiancé and setting his mother up to take the fall."

"That was your earring I found in her bedroom, wasn't it?" I couldn't believe everything he was saying. He'd seemed so normal.

He touched his ear. "I wondered where that went."

"If you already killed Ariana, I don't get why you killed the widow?" I kept him talking while I looked around, still trying to figure my way out of this situation.

"When I heard Ariana had lied about the baby and being Steven's fiancé, I felt cheated. I was furious. I still hadn't gotten my revenge."

"You came to his house to kill me, didn't you?" Chloe said, her voice sounding so disappointed. "And to think I recommended you to all my friends. Your mother would be ashamed."

"My mother is dead."

"Did you kill her, too?" Chloe pursed her lips in disapproval.

"No." He frowned. "Never mind about that. Where was I?" He shifted his weight. "Ah yes, that stupid widow woman grew a conscience. She said she wanted to apologize to you, but she saw me in your house. I couldn't let her live and tell everyone, so I dragged her out back and hit her over the head with the only thing I could find."

"The pooper scooper," I said. "That's really disgusting, by the way." I was trying to say anything to distract him.

"What?" His face looked comical in his confusion. "Whatever." He swiped a hand through the air, growing agitated. "It was the only thing I could find."

"And you knew people would think it was Chloe again."

"I hoped so, but this town has too many Greeks. You're all way too loyal to each other." His face grew angrier.

"And you still didn't have your revenge," I said, my mind whirling as it put all the pieces of the puzzle together. "You came after me because you realized I'm the person Nik cares about the most."

"Bingo." His eyes filled with intensity.

"If you wanted to kill me, then why save me after you hit me over the head?"

"I wanted to toy with you a bit." His lips curled. "Make Detective Stevens suffer a little more. Same with the fire. When you hurt, he hurts. I liked that."

Realization dawned. "You were the one following me all along, weren't you?"

"I always had eyes on you, even when you didn't sense me, but I'm through playing." He took a step toward us and clenched his fists.

Chloe let out an ear-piercing scream. "I don't want to die."

He jerked back for a moment, looking startled. He didn't have a weapon. Only his hands. Shelly said it didn't matter how big they were, you could always take someone down with proper technique.

"You don't have to do this," I raised my voice, standing in a ready position. Chloe recognized what I was doing and stood beside me in the same position.

Gabe looked at us both and just laughed, advancing another step.

"This is your last chance. We won't say anything. You can leave now, and no one will ever know."

"I would know." He growled. "I'm not leaving until I finish getting my revenge this time."

He lunged forward, while Chloe and I pushed him back and forth between us like a ping pong ball, but it wasn't quite working. This time I screamed, knowing exactly what would happen. I yelled a command to Chloe, and we both spun out of the way just in time.

Right on cue the back screen door came crashing down on top of Gabe. He let out a grunt, and Wolfgang's growl was much more menacing than anything Gabe could do.

"Get this monster off me," Gabe wheezed in barely more than a whisper. "I can't breathe. He belongs in a cage."

"*You're* the monster," Chloe said.

"Wolf, ease up and stay," I said.

Wolfgang shifted just enough so Gabe could breathe, yet contained him. My little deputy. Okay, big deputy. Either way, he deserved a reward. I patted him on the head. He licked my hand, and I only cringed a little before running over to my phone to call the police.

Hearing the sirens wail in the background moments later, I stared Gabe in the eye and said, "The only place you're going is right back to *your* cage where you belong."

EPILOGUE

Nik pulled out my chair at Rosalita's Place, and I sat down as he pushed the chair back in. He took a seat next to me at a small, romantic table in the corner, and I could smell the alluring essence that was strictly Detective Dreamy.

"I thought it fitting our first official date be at the place where we first met." He smiled at me, looking almost shy.

"That's so sweet," I said, suddenly nervous. I wiped off the edge of my water glass and took a sip of my water.

He did the same and loosened his tie. He looked as nervous as I felt, and that made me feel better than anything he could have said.

"Detective Johnson called earlier. Gabe Scarlatta is back in prison where he belongs." Nik let out a heavy sigh. "I can't believe I missed that. Here I was looking into Ma's past and Ariana's past. I never thought to look into my own. I put you all in danger without even realizing it. I should have been more thorough."

"You're a great detective, Nik. Even Darnell didn't

recognize him. Using a different name and changing his appearance that drastically would fool even Sherlock Holmes." I smiled, trying to lighten the mood. "I should have known Erik was a bad guy when he used non-organic fertilizer. I had a talk with Yanni to put an end to that asap."

"Speaking of missing things. I can't believe those sweet ladies were the Business Bandits, and awkward Rex transformed into a confident special agent. He deserves an Oscar for that performance." I laughed and took a sip of water. "I'm just so glad we got your ma's heirloom necklace back."

"Me too." He shook his head. "That's in a safe where it belongs. Ma finally agreed now that she knows how much it's worth."

A couple walked in and sat at a table across the room. I waved at Nelson and Milly.

"Who would have thought they would hit it off so well?" Nik said in wonder.

"I did." I gave him a devilish smile. "Just like I knew my cousin Silas and the bartender Zena would hit it off. He asked her out on an actual date. That's huge for him."

"Guess he's finally met his match."

"We'll see." I lifted a shoulder. "We'll also see if your ma and Captain Crenshaw are a good match."

"I can't even go there." Nik winced.

"Well, you don't have a choice. He asked her out again, and she finally forgave him enough to say yes."

Nik groaned in protest, and I giggled.

"You'll be okay, big guy."

"Speaking of couples, my man Boomer finally asked Jaz to move in with him. I wonder if she'll say yes."

"She already did."

Nik's brows shot up. "She did? He'll be so happy. He was worried she wouldn't agree to move out, and I was worried if he moved in, you would be homeless. What's she going to do with her half of the house?"

"Now that I make enough from my lingerie line, I'm renting the half by myself," I said proudly. "This is the first time I've lived on my own. I'm actually excited."

"And I'm right next door if you need to borrow a cup of sugar."

I laughed out loud at that one. "Um, no offense, but I would trust my baking supplies over yours any day."

"Speaking of lingerie and couples and moving in together...can we start over?"

"I thought you'd never ask."

We both let out a nervous breath and then laughed, finally relaxing.

"Welcome back, Kalli." Detective Stevens took my hand and then kissed my cheek, in a full-circle moment. He was so handsome. Tall with thick, wavy, coffee-colored hair, olive skin and a heavily whiskered face. His piercing blue eyes twinkled before he leaned in to whisper, "I missed you," into my ear. *If you give me a chance, I'll be happy to show you just how much.*

"I missed you, too," I said like before, only this time I added, "Yes."

"Are you reading my mind, or something?" He winked.

"Or something." I winked back, happier than I had been in a very long time. *He's going to marry you some day*, whispered through my mind. Maybe someday I would be saying *yes* to another question. A vision of the future flashed before my eyes.

"What's wrong?" he asked curiously. "You have a funny look on your face."

A slow smile tipped up the corners of my lips at the premonition I'd just had. "Absolutely nothing for once," I said and meant it.

My future was looking very bright indeed.

This series, and especially this book, are dedicated to my best friends who are also Book Cents Babes and my critique partners. Barbara Witek and Danielle LaBue are the most inspiring, motivating, talented, best brainstorming, most fun badass bitches I know. I could seriously not do ANY of this without them. Love you both so much and can't wait to be doing this for another twenty years!

ABOUT THE AUTHOR

Kari Lee Townsend is a National Bestselling Author of mysteries & a tween superhero series. She also writes romance and women's fiction as Kari Lee Harmon. With a background in English education, she's now a full-time writer, wife to her own superhero, mom of 3 sons, 1 darling diva, 1 daughter-in-law & 2 lovable fur babies. These days you'll find her walking her dogs or hard at work on her next story, living a blessed life.

ALSO BY THE AUTHOR

Two Cents of Doom (Kalli Ballas Mystery #2)

Mind Over Murder (Kalli Ballas Mystery #1)

Harmful Habits (Cece Monroe Mystery #1)

Murder in the Meditation (Sunny Meadows Mystery #8)

Chaos and Cold Feet (Sunny Meadows Mystery short story #7)

Hazard in the Horoscope (Sunny Meadows Mystery #6)

Perish in the Palm (Sunny Meadows Mystery #5)

Shenanigans in the Shadows (Sunny Meadows Mystery short story #4)

Trouble in the Tarot (Sunny Meadows Mystery #3)

Corpse in the Crystal Ball (Sunny Meadows Mystery #2)

Tempest in the Tea Leaves (Sunny Meadows Mystery #1)

Valley of Secrets

Until Tomorrow

Jingle all the Way (Merry Scroog-mas novella #3)

Sleigh Bells Ring (Merry Scroog-mas novella #2)

Naughty or Nice (Merry Scroog-mas novella #1)

Brook (Lakehouse Treasures novella #4)

Meghan (Lakehouse Treasure novella #3)

Amber (Lakehouse Treasures novella #2)

The Beginning (Lakehouse Treasures novella #1)

Sleeping in the Middle (Comfort Club #1)

Love Lessons
Project Produce

Spurred by Fate (Triple R Ranch short story #2)
Destiny Wears Spurs (Triple R Ranch #1)

CPSIA information can be obtained
at www.ICGtesting.com
Printed in the USA
LVHW091749110622
721067LV00013B/407